GOOD WATER

GOOD WATER

KAYT C. PECK

SAPPHIRE BOOKS

SALINAS, CALIFORNIA

Dedication

To a horse named Jack Seven and a dog called Big Mack. They were a big part of my adult life on the ranch and dear memories of those two helped motivate me to write Good Water.

Chapter One

The noise tore through the darkness like a knife through the heart. Judy groped toward the nightstand, knocking the blaring alarm onto its back, before she found the button and strangled the clock into silence.

She collapsed onto the bed and dug at her eyes with the heels of her hands, trying to fight through sleepy haze to normal vision. She'd had a bad night, a short night, but then they always were before shipping.

A breeze fluttered at the curtains over the open window. Judy leaned outside the warm cocoon of the covers to lift back the curtain and look outside. Black as…midnight? No, Judy didn't agree with that. If she were to adhere to any cliché, it would be the old "darkest before the dawn." She knew that dark. She'd known it at least twice a year since she was old enough to ride drag on an aging cutting horse. A cowhand always rose before sunup on shipping day.

Within a few hours, Judy would harvest the fruit of months of labor. Her grass fed steers would be on their way to a feedlot, and she'd have her check. *Good. There are bills to pay.*

She reached for the clock and set it upright. The digital 4:45 glared red and angry at her. She didn't blame it. Anger was a natural reaction to that hour of the morning.

Judy figured she'd had three hours sleep…maybe

three and a half. She was feeling a might red and angry herself. Sure, she'd gone to bed early, but she never slept well before shipping. There were so many things that could go wrong. Rain might turn the roads into a quagmire so that the trucks couldn't fight their way down the dirt path to the corrals. There could be a fence down and cattle from here to Dallas. Most of all, no one could ever know what the dadblamed cattle would do.

Judy spent most of her life working with and learning to read the ways of cattle. *Cattle...good God, cattle. How can anything so stupid be so unpredictable? Seems like beefsteak on the hoof is all instinct and spontaneity. If they choose today as a time to run, I might well lose thousands of dollars.* The weight expended in unnecessary exercise converted directly into lost profits, when the animals hit the feedlot scales.

The clock glared its red 4:50.

Five precious minutes lost, thinking on the stupidity of cattle.

The house was quiet, too quiet. A cricket sang outside, but the morning birds were not yet awake. Judy missed the noise of her father and mother in the next room. She missed the heavy sound of her father's boots as they hit the floor. That thud had been a sign that it was time to get up, that mother would have breakfast ready soon, and there was work to do. No boot thud, no smell of breakfast...just a memory.

She hadn't heard those boots on the hardwood floor for two years, and she never would again. Her father was buried in them. Nor would she smell the aroma of her mother's homemade biscuits. Her mother rested in a grave beside him, sharing the same tombstone. The irrevocable car accident killed her parents and called Judy back home. There was a ranch to run and only her to do it.

Judy tried to laugh.

"You always do turn morbid when you don't get enough sleep," Judy mumbled to herself.

The woman shuffled along in her cotton nightshirt, until she reached the kitchen. Her hand touched the electric switch and a harsh, white light overpowered the dark. Judy's hands flew to her face in a momentary defense against the invasion of brightness. She squinted with one eye, the other safely closed, as she flicked the on switch to the coffeemaker. The device was already filled with water and coffee. Judy had done everything possible the previous night, before her brain and body were sleep fouled.

As the water heated, she lifted the lid on an electric CrockPot. The smell of pinto beans would be welcome by the time she served a late lunch to all her volunteer hands. In the early morning air, the odor left Judy slightly nauseous. She retrieved one of the last jars of her mother's pickled jalapeños from the refrigerator. Holding the jar at arm's length, she selected a pepper and plopped it whole into the beans. The jalapeño would be retrieved from the pot before serving. It was fine for spicing, but an accidental bite into that fruit could incapacitate a cowboy. Not a good way to thank helpful neighbors.

A quick glance, as she reopened the refrigerator to return the jalapeños, assured Judy that the Pyrex trays of cornbread batter were ready for the oven. Cornbread and beans weren't much compared to the feasts Judy enjoyed when she neighbored at the Bar D or the HaskinsBoyles Ranch, but the meal was the best she could do on this ranch, where she was both father and mother, man and woman.

Back in the bedroom, it didn't take long for Judy to dress in worn jeans and a chambray work shirt. The coffee was done when she returned to the kitchen. Breakfast was a fast cup, black, and two cold biscuits with peanut butter and jelly. It was still pitch-black when Judy shrugged on her jacket and jammed her head into her sweat stained Resistol. As she stepped outside, an adrenaline powered rush of excitement replaced her earlier exhaustion.

Useless set up a fit of barking, while Somegood slinked quietly by the other dog's side. The two animals had been awakened from a warm sleep, nestled in the loose straw in the barn.

"Useless, get over here," Judy called.

A burr filled wad of brown fur stopped barking at the sound of her mistress's voice, but the bitch, of very questionable heritage, didn't come immediately. Instead, the medium sized cocker/collie/pug/coyote (maybe)/mostanythingcanine tucked her tail between her legs and lay rooted to the ground.

"I know you don't like it, but it's got to be done."

The dog slunk reluctantly toward the shed side door Judy held open. Judy snapped her fingers and pointed. Chastised, Useless went inside. Somegood started to follow, but Judy pushed the border collie gently outside.

"Not you, Somegood. We've both got work to do."

Judy stepped inside the shed and assured herself that there was food and water for the little brown dog.

"Don't look so sad eyed, Useless. If I left you out on gathering day, we'd likely both end up shot. You'd be scattering cattle from here to Christmas."

Judy turned out the light and closed the door. For a few minutes, a plaintive whine came from the shed, but it soon stopped. Useless liked the sympathy, but she knew a good thing when she had it, time for more sleep.

A sickly, yellow light emitted from the lone lightbulb, illuminating the retired railroad boxcar that served as tack room for the Handle P ranch, the place her grandfather had homesteaded more than eighty years earlier. Judy took her shotgun chaps from the nail where they hung near the door, and stepped awkwardly into the narrow legs without bothering to unzip them. She took a bridle from the wall and carried it back into the cool of the morning.

The horses heard the activity. All three nickered from the corrals, curious and hoping for an early morning snack. The hint of light over the horizon outlined two geldings' heads over the edge of the corrals.

"Morning Jackson," Judy said to her own baldfaced sorrel. "Morning Big Tom," she added to her father's bay.

The bay didn't get ridden much anymore, but Judy couldn't bring herself to sell him when she had sold the majority of her father's breeding quarter horses. Working alone, she didn't have time to keep up with the horse breeding operation, especially the breaking of the colts. Besides, it was a task she had never much enjoyed. She kept one broodmare. Sally Doc Bar, heavy with foal, watched patiently from the adjacent pen.

"Hey, Miss Sally," Judy called as she climbed the fence.

Judy thought briefly of the foal the mare carried, sired by Poco Leo, it was bound to be a good foal. Faithful Jackson had just turned twelve. Once the colt was broken and trained, it would give the aging saddle horse some welcome relief.

At the moment, Jackson was acting more like a two-year-old. Judy maneuvered the gelding into one corner of the corral. His ears lay threateningly against his head, as he turned his back end toward her, halfheartedly threatening to kick.

"Don't you give me that, mister. You know better."

Judy watched his hind legs for the kick she didn't really expect to come. She walked confidently to Jackson's side and down to his shoulder. His ears eased forward as she scratched under his jaw, the place that always itched, but he never seemed able to scratch. Judy eased the reins around his neck and then placed the headstall over his head. The brief rebellion passed. The gelding chewed the bit into his mouth, just as she had trained him nine years ago. She'd used nearly a whole jar of molasses getting the job done, but it was a lesson he never forgot.

Jackson followed her easily, back to the boxcar. Judy dropped the reins, trusting in her gelding's training to keep him in place as she currycombed his back, sides, and stomach. It was too dark to really see what she was doing. She hoped that the comb was catching any stray cockleburs. If any were left, she'd find out soon enough after she swung into the saddle.

Jackson stood quietly, as she lifted the saddle onto his back and tightened the cinches, first front, then back. She fastened the breast collar and checked to make sure her catch rope was held in place by the rawhide thong on the saddle horn.

In the distance, Judy could see the lights of an approaching vehicle. *It must be Brad and Harold Kenton. They are always the first to arrive, their horses saddled and trailered, ready to start the day's work.* Judy just had time to ride out and open the south gate into the catch pen, leading to the corrals. She led Jackson a few steps, just to make sure the saddle was settled into place, and then climbed to a seat that was as natural to her as the living room couch.

Once she'd gone through the outside gate to the catch pen, opening and closing the gate from horseback, she urged Jackson into a trot toward the wire gate separating the pen from the main pasture. The world around her changed from black to grey and there was a hint of color in the east. After she opened the gate, Judy remounted and started the ride back.

From long years of practice, she and Jackson were already moving in perfect harmony. The sun came up.

Yellow, red, and gold filled the sky. The last of the morning birds awoke from their slumber and sent their music for the whole world to hear. The smell in the air, found only on the morning prairie, spoke of promise, hope, and a still sweet life. Judy felt the horse move beneath her and was at one...not just with the horse, but with the universe.

Judy pulled Jackson to a halt, just as the Kenton pickup and trailer rattled to a standstill on the other side of the fence.

"Damn it, woman," Brad Kenton called through the open window of the pickup. "Anybody with a grin like that, this time of the morning, has got to be out of her mind."

"Welcome to the funny farm."

"At least we got a happy boss for the day's work," Brad answered.

His father pushed the pickup door open. The door gave an angry squeak from too much dust and not enough oil.

"Let's just hope the grin lasts through the day," Harold Kenton added.

A frown touched at Judy's eyes.

"That'll depend on the cattle, and our own luck," she said.

"Good luck or bad?" Brad asked.

"Time will tell."

Chapter Two

Judy scrubbed at her hands with the bar of forever filthy Lava soap she kept hidden under the sink, in an equally filthy soap dish. It was a habit she had inherited from her mother, who had given up on keeping the heavy-duty hand soap presentable. Dirty hands were a hazard of ranch life. Dirty work made dirty hands, and dirty hands tainted the soap that cleaned them.

"I appreciate you coming over to help," Judy said as she scrubbed.

"Just being neighborly," Martha Kenton answered.

The woman's presence was more than that, and Judy knew it. There was a time, when Judy was still too small to know exactly how things were supposed to be, when she believed she and Brad each had two mothers. Martha Kenton and Collette Proctor had been best friends.

Being best friends did not mean shopping for clothes together, giving opinions on color and cut. They were best friends who sensed the other's tears before they were cried. Best friends meant nurturing each other's children, as if they were their own. Best friends meant nurturing each other's dreams as if they were their own.

Judy looked at her second mother and figured the pain would never go away for Martha Kenton. Aware that every minute Martha spent in the Proctor home was filled with bittersweet memories, Judy hoped that the older woman could sense her gratitude. Being at the Handle P was painful for Martha, but here she was, despite the pain, all because Judy needed her. Martha still nurtured Collette's children as if they were her own.

Judy scrubbed down to the skin, as the dirt washed down the drain in grey rivulets. Outside, the men hunkered down under a shade tree, drinking the beer Judy had kept hidden in a cooler until the work was done. As she rinsed the last of the soap, the cool well water felt good against her skin. Judy looked at her hands and smiled. They looked ludicrously white against the dusty layer on her arms and clothing. At least they were clean enough to handle the food. Judy filled a glass and drank deeply. She closed her eyes and enjoyed the feel as her hot and thirsty body soaked up the moisture.

"God, you've got good water." Judy heard Sandy's voice.

The voice was crystal clear. Amazing considering Judy hadn't heard it for over a year.

Comes straight out of the Ogallala Aquifer, 600 feet down. Judy's voice echoed in her own mind.

Judy held her eyes shut. She didn't want the memory to end.

Sandy had stood beside her in this very kitchen. The stolen moment alone, Judy's fingers intertwined with her lover's, was the first moment of happiness she had known since the phone call with the shattering news of her parents' deaths.

"I can certainly understand why you love it here," Sandy had said as she watched the setting sun turn the prairie into one of God's watercolors.

But she hadn't understood.

"You can't stay here, Judy," Sandy yelled.

"I can't go."

"We've got a life."

"I can't go."

"Well, I will!"

Pregnant silence.

"Then go."

There were tears. Sandy left. There were more tears. Then the heifers had calved. Judy didn't cry as much then. New life had a way of making one forget pain and feel hope instead.

"How'd the gathering go?"

Martha Kenton's voice hauled Judy back to the present.

"Pretty good. Cattle didn't break but once, and we managed to get 'em slowed before they scattered. Came out three long on the count, though."

"I'd rather come out long than short. It's easier to return the neighbor's cattle than find lost ones of your own," Martha responded.

"Unfortunately, we found four Bar D steers as we were loading the trucks. I'm still one short."

"We'd all get worried if life was too easy."

Judy crossed to the table. Martha had already laid out bowls, spoons, and plates. The cowhands would gather their food and then go back outside, returning to the beer and the shade trees as they ate.

"Sure does look good, Martha," Judy said as she admired the table.

The simple meal of beans and cornbread expanded noticeably when Martha arrived. A heaping bowl of German potato salad rested on one end of the table, the top covered by a tea towel to keep the flies from 'lighting. Judy heard her stomach grumble, as she lifted the lid on a plastic bowl and saw the generous portion of homegrown cucumbers and onions, freshly sliced and soaking in a concoction of vinegar and water. Martha stood guard over two pies hiding on the kitchen counter, one apple and one coconut cream, both baked just that morning.

Judy crossed to the oven and gently opened the door. Brad's mother must have watched from the back window as the crew loaded cattle. When the last truck filled, the bread went into the oven. Judy had watched her own mother use the same trick.

Judy smiled past the fatigue. It was proving to be a good day.

"Why don't you marry my boy?"

The feeling of wellbeing froze somewhere between Judy's heart and her stomach. She turned to face Martha. Judy noticed the lines of strain around the older woman's eyes. Yes, it was still difficult for Martha Kenton to visit the home of her best friend… her dead friend.

"Martha, I—"

"It's just not right, you living here alone. What…" there was a crack in her voice, "What would your mother say?"

"She'd say 'do what you gotta do, Judy girl.'"

"In a pig's eye," Martha answered.

Judy felt a flush of anger. "Martha, I appreciate all you've done for me, but you have to remember, I'm a grown woman."

There was a hint of tears in her eyes as Martha leaned close to Judy and placed her hand on the younger woman's arm.

"You're also the daughter of a woman who meant more to me than anybody else. What she'd want is for you to be happy. She'd want it, and I want it."

"I am happy."

"How can you be? You don't have anybody."

"Come on, Martha. You spend days at a time alone in this emptiness, while your men are out working. I swear, there are birds out here who won't sing if there's more than one pair of ears listening. I got work I love and a whole universe, in the pastures and prairie around me."

The sun inflicted wrinkles around Martha's eyes creased with the intensity of her expression.

"It don't mean nothing if there's nobody to care."

Judy waved a dramatic hand toward the carefully set table and the food that rested there. "You care. Brad and Harold care. Craig cares."

"Craig?" Martha made a noise like a swallowed hurumph. "That brother of yours is too wrapped up in computers to care what happens to you."

"He's got a right to his own life."

"So do you."

"I have a life. The life I want."

"But you're alone!"

"No. I'm not."

Martha's breath carried the slight scent of vinegar as she leaned close. The woman had sampled the cucumbers.

"Girl, you've never been married. You don't know what it's like to wake up in the night and feel a warm body beside you…to hear the rhythm of his breathing."

Unbidden, the familiar scent of Sandy's skin

erupted in full blossom, a hint of vanilla from the shampoo she always used. Judy closed her eyes and, for an instant, she could feel the tickle of Sandy's freshly washed hair against her face.

"Say what you like," Martha continued. "You'll always be alone, until there's a set of arms to hold you and willing ears to listen at the end of the day."

Judy turned away to hide her pain. "None of us can have everything, Martha. There's a price to pay for all our choices."

Martha took Judy's arm and turned the younger woman to face her.

"Why pay this price, Judy girl?"

Judy looked long and hard into her second mother's eyes. The truth danced on the edge of her tongue, then it was gone.

"I can't explain, Martha. It's just too complicated."

"But—"

"Good Lord! The cornbread!"

The two women turned in mild panic, as Judy pulled the oven door open. The cornbread was on the brown side, but still acceptable, especially to a hungry bunch of cowhands.

"Time to eat," Judy said.

"We'll talk more, later," Martha responded.

Judy retreated out the back door. Useless rose from her customary cool spot beneath the porch and joined her mistress on the walk across the yard. The dog couldn't stand to be parted from Judy's side after spending a morning locked in the shed.

"Useless, next time Martha gets me cornered like that, I want you to come to my rescue."

The dog stared upward in adoration.

"Right. Just don't forget."

Judy stopped by the old-fashioned metal triangle that hung from the back fence. She took an oversized bolt from where it rested on the fence and banged the metal against the inside edges of the triangle. Any cowhand from the past 150 years would have recognized that tuneless music. It was time for dinner.

Chapter Three

The shocks on the pickup gave a mild groan, as the last sack of Horse and Mule was thrown atop the rest of the feed.

"That all for you today, Miss Proctor?"

"Reckon so, Duey," Judy answered the young man. Duey smiled warmly at Judy, as she stood in the pickup bed.

The two worked together, loading mineral blocks and horse feed, with the quiet ease of those familiar with their job. As Duey passed up blocks and feed sacks, Judy transferred the load to a newly formed stack that she would restack yet again once she got home. There'd be no smiling Duey to help her with that job. She didn't mind. Hell, she didn't even think about it. The lift and load of fifty pound bags of horse feed was just another part of her life.

Judy jumped from the pickup. She and Duey walked through the cool, sweet smell of molasses soaked feed. As a child, Judy loved going with her father to the feed store. There was something about the orderly rows of neatly stacked feed that convinced her there was something right about life. Besides, she'd had a special fondness for Moreman's Feed chewing gum. The little boxes were miniature replicas of salt block packages. As a child, she'd always assumed the cattle liked the salt blocks so much because they tasted like the chewing gum. She believed that until the day she stuck her tongue to one of the blocks. That was a disillusion—and a taste—she'd never forget.

Judy browsed over the tack, enjoying the smell of new leather, as Duey completed the feed ticket.

"How's everything going out at the ranch?" Duey asked.

"Fine. Got the yearlings gathered and shipped a couple of weeks ago."

"That's always a relief."

Judy stepped forward and signed the ticket. She smiled and gestured toward the document in front of her.

"Especially for those I owe money."

"We never worry about you, Miss Proctor. Just like we never worried about your dad."

"Thank you, Duey. That's good to hear."

The pickup rode at a burdened angle, as she drove out the double door and bumped her way onto Highway 54. Judy didn't even hear the moans and groans of the overburdened shock absorbers. There wasn't a cowhand around without a few aches, nor a ranch pickup without a few squeaks.

Judy enjoyed the simple business of her Fridays in town. The brief visits were an essential line to the rest of life, to a world where people cared about fashion, and knew the art of doing lunch. That was the world she had known and left. She instead chose to return to the tiny ecosystem of her childhood, to the realness of it. Judy choked and smothered on the artificiality of the city. The only real truth she had found in her time there had been the truth about herself... the truth about her sexual orientation. The city had given her someone to love.

The flashing green of Sandy's eyes teased Judy's

memory, and she could almost hear the laughter. Her persistent regret was tempered with the certainty that had carried her through the past two years. *This is home. I belong here.*

Of its own accord, the pickup passed Walmart and turned right at the Y that led toward downtown, through the railroad underpass, and opened to the bustle of Main Street. Judy returned to the present when a friendly driver honked as he passed, going the opposite direction. At a glance, Judy recognized the teenaged son of one of her neighbors.

As she drove past Ben Franklin's, City Drug, and Watson's Western Wear, a smile played over Judy's face. The sun wrinkles at the corners of her eyes gave her a sparkle of youth and an aura of wisdom, and left more than one person mystified as to her age. Judy loved the sights and sounds of Main Street. They didn't give her the same feelings of peace and belonging as the call of a killdeer or the sight of antelope grazing nearby, but they came as close as most anything else… except maybe the sound of Sandy's rhythmic breathing in the bed beside her.

Judy shook her head in a vain attempt to clear her thoughts.

"What's with me these days?" she mumbled.

Not long after she returned to Dulson County, Judy had decided that she was alone and would, most likely, always be alone. Thoughts of Sandy were something she held sacred for special moments. If nurtured too often, they became more pain than pleasure.

There were two parking spaces in the same block as the office. Judy needed them both. With the stack of feed in the back of the pickup, it was difficult to see behind her.

Judy plunked her quarter in the parking meter, one of the same parking meters that had served her hometown for over thirty years, and made her way to the newsroom of the *City Gazette*. At least, most folks called it the newsroom. The advertising and production offices were all piled in the same place, but the town still thought of it as the newsroom. It was a name that came out of the thirties, when a big city fellow spent five years as managing editor. He'd always called it the newsroom, and most folks complied just to keep him happy. Nobody much remembered the long-gone editor, but the town still called it the newsroom.

The musty smell of water-cooled air conditioning had a welcome feel to it, as Judy walked into the office that had served as the town's newspaper since 1910. It had changed some over the years, but there was still the pressed tin ceiling and the ongoing attempt to keep up with the everyday drama of life in a small town. The names changed, but the life was perennial. Judy loved that solidity about her home.

"Speak of the devil," a familiar voice called from the back of the room.

Judy walked to the same desk she walked to almost every Friday. Lunch with Deb Monroe was a highlight of her week. It felt strange at first, spending time with the friend of her childhood who was no longer a child. Deb too had left their home for an education in the city, but it had been the love of a man, not the land, that brought her home. She'd stepped into her job as a reporter at the *Gazette* right after college, and she'd continued on through two children and one promotion. For most of the town, Deb was the news. She was the one you told it to and the one you read it from.

For Judy, Deb was the one she told her thoughts.

Deb was the only one who knew about Sandy... about a lot of things. The important part of news reporting was knowing what news to keep to one's self. Judy knew Deb was good at it.

"We've been talking about you," Deb said.

Judy glanced at the stranger sitting in the interview seat. She caught a quick impression of brown hair and soft denim. Not the work-worn kind, but the denim that starts out soft, stonewashed right at the factory.

"And I thought it was the sun making my ears burn," Judy responded.

"Judy, meet Kathleen Romero. She's a freelance writer, working for *Cosmopolitan*," Deb said. Judy's eyebrows raised noticeably. "Yeah, I was impressed, too."

"Nice to meet you," Judy responded as she proffered a hand.

The woman stood and took the hand in a firm handshake. She did not decrease her grip as the smoothness of her hand met Judy's calluses.

"Kathleen, this is the Judy Proctor I was telling you about."

"Nice to meet you," the city woman responded. Her voice was soft, yet strong, like her hand.

"Kathleen's on assignment for an article about the women of today's West. She's wanting to get to know life on the range, face to face."

Deb leaned back with the air of ease that led so many people to tell her more than they should.

"She's wanting to spend some time on a ranch, and I was telling her that you are the one she needs to see. How would you feel about her staying out at your place?"

Judy turned to study the stranger. She saw city written on both clothes and face.

"It can get awful lonely out in the boondocks," Judy responded.

"That's part of what I'm here to learn and write about," Kathleen said.

"Think on it," Deb said. She looked at the clock on the wall. "Judy girl, the paper's put to bed, and I'm ready for lunch."

"J & S enchiladas?"

"You got it. Grab your stuff, Kathleen. We'll introduce you to the Mexican food that keeps the country girls coming to town."

"Does me, that's for sure," Judy added.

The three trooped outside, and Deb led a direct route to Judy's pickup.

"Where you going?" Judy asked. "Let's take your car."

"Kathleen wants to experience life on the range." Deb opened the passenger door and looked dubiously at the upholstery, as she moved the coffee can full of fencing staples and the electric fence tester.

"Hope you don't mind starting with a good sample of Useless and Somegood hair," Deb added.

"Useless and Somegood?" Kathleen asked.

"I'll explain over lunch," Judy answered.

Judy felt breathless as she walked around the pickup to take the driver's seat. There was a pleasant feeling of unreality mixed with a not so pleasant sense of being out of control as she started the engine. *Damn, I wish Deb would warn me about these things,* she thought as the pickup creaked away from the curb. She thought she could detect a flash of apprehension in the city woman's eyes as Kathleen glanced in the mirror at the loaded pickup bed. Judy could feel the woman's doubts about the reliability of the vehicle.

"Don't worry. My old truck will make it," Judy assured the stranger.

"And if she doesn't, we don't have far to walk," Deb added.

Deb ignored Judy's warning glare as the veteran newswoman launched into a tale of a local rancher, who said that all a four-wheel drive pickup was good for was getting him farther from the house before he got stuck. Judy decided it was going to be a very long lunch.

Chapter Four

The conversation took place over the World's Greatest Enchiladas. Judy didn't even have teeth when she ate the first of what would prove to be thousands of the World's Greatest Enchiladas.

Her father had cut away a third of one from his plate and placed it on the tray of her highchair…a tray already smeared with guacamole and Gerber's peaches. All in all, it had made a colorful mess. It had also started Judy's addiction to the Mexican food at J & S. During one of the three visits Sandy had made after Judy returned to the ranch, she had accused Judy of coming back home just because she couldn't live without J & S enchiladas.

It had been an attempt at humor, but the pain hidden behind the words took all the laughter away. That was Sandy's last visit and one of their last meals together. For a long time Judy hadn't returned to J & S, but not even the pain of Sandy's parting could keep Judy away from the World's Greatest Enchiladas.

It wasn't just Judy who gave a title to the concoction of corn tortillas, meat, tomatoes, and chilies. Most all of Dulson County agreed. When family and friends came from out-of-state, J & S enchiladas were high on the list of local tourist attractions.

Judy remained silent about her secret belief that the title of World's Greatest Enchilada really belonged to a local fast food restaurant in El Paso, Texas. She and Sandy had stopped at Taco Casa during a trip to West Texas, when Sandy had a job interview.

Judy dared not confess that she had found a better enchilada. The whole town would be miffed. If she told the full truth, she could be burned at the stake.

The El Paso enchiladas were chicken, not something one confessed in cattle country.

"These are very good," Kathleen said as she finished her first bite of enchilada.

"You better say more than that, dear. Here in Dulson County, we think these are the World's Greatest Enchiladas," Deb answered as she offered the visitor a basket filled with mighty fine sopapillas (they didn't quite merit an official title).

Kathleen's brow creased in thought.

"I'm not sure," she said.

"What? You don't like them!" Deb was shocked.

"No, no. They're excellent. It's just that, well, have you ever been to El Paso?"

Judy inhaled tea halfway up her nose, and then spent thirty seconds trying to choke to death as quietly as possible. Deb thumped her on the back and chastised her old friend for trying to drown.

"I'm…(cough, sputter)…all…(cough, cough)…right," Judy insisted.

Kathleen said nothing. It was a simple touch. The city woman placed her hand briefly over Judy's and looked at the country woman with a sympathy so intense, that Judy found herself breathing just because of the comfort she saw in those eyes.

Kathleen took her hand away, and Judy felt cold and lonely.

"You gonna' live?" Deb asked with mock

harshness.

"I told you I was all right."

"Good, our enchiladas are getting cold." Deb dug into her own lunch with enthusiasm. "Don't let my friend's eating technique deceive you, Kathleen," Deb said, pausing briefly between bites. "She is actually quite civilized. College educated and the whole nine yards."

Deb turned her attention back to the food.

"Where did you go to school?" Kathleen asked.

Judy looked at her plate. She consciously collected herself from her unexpected reaction to the city visitor's touch.

"Texas Tech in Lubbock."

"Good school. What did you study?"

"Art education."

"Instead of teaching, you came back to the ranch?"

"No, I taught for a couple of years, and then I went into commercial art."

"Here?" Kathleen asked, obviously surprised.

"Lord no. In Dallas."

"Ranching is quite a change from art."

Judy looked intently at Kathleen.

"Maybe in the working environment. Maybe in the bank account. But not in the heart. For me, art and ranching live side by side."

Kathleen met Judy's gaze, and Judy received yet another shock. The city woman understood. Judy could see it in her eyes.

"Kathleen, take some advice from a smalltown editor," Deb said.

"What?"

Deb pointed at Kathleen's nearly untouched

enchiladas. "Don't ever let an interview get in the way of lunch."

The three women laughed.

Obediently, Kathleen and Judy turned to their own meals in an attempt to finish at the same time as Deb. It was hopeless. Deb was already eating her second sopapilla with honey by the time the other two women finished their main meal. All three ordered coffee as the waitress hauled away their empty plates.

"You two sure aren't doing much talking," Deb said.

"Every time we do, you tell us to start eating," Judy responded.

"You're finished eating now, aren't you?"

"Better be. My plate's gone."

"So talk."

There was immediate silence. Each woman looked expectantly at the others until they broke out in spontaneous giggles.

"Why is it the one time it's impossible to think of something to say is when someone demands that you say something? When I'm doing interviews, all I have to do to get someone to shut up is turn on the digital recorder. They look at it like they're hypnotized," Deb said.

"I know what you mean," Kathleen responded. "The first thing you have to do in any interview is to get the subject to forget it's an interview."

"Lord, Deb, you and I shouldn't have any trouble finding things to say to each other," Judy said.

"No kidding. We survived puberty together. Nothing should stand between us."

"Miss Crawley thought we had too much to say to each other in seventh grade."

"We sure spent enough time standing at the front of the class holding an unabridged dictionary in each hand," Deb recalled.

"I guess Miss Crawley wanted us to realize how weighty language can be," Judy said.

Kathleen laughed and Deb moaned.

"Judy, girl. You been living alone too long."

The teasing statement hit Judy like a slap. *What's wrong with me today?*

"Maybe you're right."

Deb tapped her friend on the shoulder. "Hey, don't go morose on me. It was just a joke."

"At least I don't groan at yours."

"I'll remember you said that," Deb threatened.

The waitress brought coffee. The three collected their thoughts as they customized their caffeine with milk and sugar. Judy turned her attention to the city woman.

"Where are you from, Kathleen?" Judy asked.

"Here and there. I more or less live in Colorado Springs."

"More or less?" Deb tipped her head with the question.

"Yes. I rent a house there, but I travel a good deal of the time."

"Like the road?" Judy asked

"Bet you don't like the loneliness," Deb said.

Judy backhanded Deb on the upper arm.

"What did I tell you? Living in the boondocks doesn't mean loneliness."

"Ouch," Deb responded.

"What does it mean…living in the boondocks, that is?" Kathleen asked.

Judy looked at the newcomer. She looked hard.

"Not yet. I don't want to be a subject yet. If you're going to be staying with me, I want to know something about you."

"Am I going to be staying with you?"

The look the two women exchanged generated a haze of heat.

"Yeah, I reckon you are, if you still want to."

Kathleen looked at Deb. "You're right. She's perfect."

"But can you handle Useless and Somegood?" Deb asked.

"What in the hell are useless and somegood?" Kathleen demanded.

"They're both the names and adjectives describing my two dogs," Judy answered.

Kathleen thought a minute and then chuckled. "I like it."

"Let's hope they like you," Judy said. "Somegood once tore a hole in the seat of a salesman's pants."

Kathleen laughed. "I'll remember to watch my back."

"And your butt. That's Somegood's favorite target," Deb commented.

"If we're going to be roomies, you'd better tell me about yourself. Where'd you go to school?"

"University of Colorado at Boulder. I majored in journalism."

"How long you been working for *Cosmo*?"

"Actually, I'm freelancing. They're just one of my clients."

Deb whistled. "Whew! That's tough, isn't it? Freelancing?"

"Sometimes. I worked for *The Denver Post* for several years, before I built up a large enough client base to strike out on my own."

"Kind of leaves you hanging out in the wind, doesn't it?"

"Like I said…sometimes, but it's worth it for the freedom."

"Sounds like ranching," Judy said.

Kathleen looked surprised. "Maybe that's why I was so drawn to this subject."

"I'll try to make it interesting."

"You already have."

❧❧❧❧

It didn't take long to unload the feed. Judy was in a hurry. She was still impatient as she placed groceries in the refrigerator and cabinets. She'd bought more than usual. After all, she was expecting company.

Normally, after her daylong visits to town, Judy would do her chores and then spend a quiet hour or two listening to music or watching television via her satellite link. Tonight, she had something else planned.

As soon as the groceries were stowed, Judy went to her office/art studio. She touched the empty drawing board and noticed with shame the layer of dust.

Sometimes she went days or even weeks without the urge to draw or paint. Today she felt an urgent desire to share the beauty she saw with her eyes and heart. It was a good feeling.

Judy sat at the drawing board and prepared the watercolors. The scene was already growing in her mind. It would be a late night for the hard working rancher.

Chapter Five

Every year, when Judy hooked the aging seed drill onto her John Deere tractor, something broke. It was rarely the same thing two years running, because Judy's repairs usually held. She'd inherited her father's fondness for welding. There was something rewarding about turning raw metal into a useful object. Sometimes, Judy thought the old drill just enjoyed the attention. To drill the three tiny patches of ground she cultivated in winter wheat took only a day or two. Repairs to the drill would fill at least a day. That ratio irritated Judy.

Although the extra income of a summer harvest was nice, Judy grew the wheat for the fresh, green grazing it gave her cattle throughout most of the winter. Trouble was, to get the winter grazing, Judy needed the cantankerous drill.

This year, the crossbar on the hitch decided it would give up the ghost. Judy managed to fill the drill and make a couple of rounds in the field near the house, before she heard the familiar groan of rending metal. She nursed the tractor and drill back to the barn, where she called to enlist Brad's assistance. He was free to help, since the Kentons hired a custom farmer for their planting. It was a prospect that sounded more and more appealing to Judy each year.

They were in the middle of welding, when a car pulled into the yard. The dogs didn't raise any kind of a ruckus. It was as though they already knew the darkhaired woman who drove her sedan, tentatively, over the rutted road.

Kathleen was curious at the flashes of light she could see within the darkened workshop. She parked her car and walked to where Judy and Brad were working, pausing only briefly to make friends with the dogs who were already wagging their welcome to the stranger. She paused to scratch the ears of the mottled mongrel.

"You must be Useless," Kathleen said.

The dog continued to smile its drooly, doggie welcome. Somegood pushed at Kathleen's fingers with his nose.

"Sorry, I didn't mean to ignore you, Somegood."

Kathleen found both hands occupied with easing the itch, always behind both dogs' ears. When she decided they'd had enough, Kathleen rose and dusted her hands against her tailored jeans. She turned her attention to the people working inside the barn.

Muscles strained and light flashed. Kathleen felt breathless at the mystery of what they were creating. She watched closely as Brad strained to aid the supports he and Judy built. He was careful that the two broken pieces of metal remained tightly abutted. When Judy finished the rough weld, he could relax a little. After the broken pieces were reunited, Judy would use C-clamps to hold additional splints to the metal, as she welded the added pieces to the frame.

Kathleen watched intently, slowly deciphering the ranchers' task. The flash of light was almost hypnotic.

From the edge of her vision, Judy noted someone approaching, but she didn't stop. This weld was too critical. If she didn't get it right the first time, it would take another two hours to reposition braces and frame. As soon as the weld attached the final centimeter of metal, she gave her head a quick jerk, flipping the welding mask to the top of her head. She looked straight into the inquisitive gaze of Kathleen's brown eyes.

"Shit," Judy said.

Brad flipped his mask to the top of his head and looked up.

"God Almighty," he said.

Kathleen was shocked and feeling very unwelcome.

"I'm sorry if you didn't know I was coming. I did try to call but…"

"How long you been watching?" Judy asked.

"A few minutes."

Judy stood so close to Kathleen that the city woman felt uncomfortable. She didn't know how to react when Judy took her chin firmly in a gloved hand and lowered Kathleen's face so that Judy could look deeply into the other woman's eyes.

"Did you look straight into the welding arc?" Brad asked as he moved to stand beside them. He pushed Judy's hand away and also grasped Kathleen by the chin and looked deeply into the stranger's eyes.

"Looked into the what?" Kathleen responded.

"The bright light," Judy answered.

"Yes."

"Shit," Judy repeated.

"Damn," Brad followed.

Kathleen was becoming alarmed.

"You should know by morning," Brad added.

Judy turned her attention from Kathleen's eyes to the woman's entire face. She read the beginnings of fear.

"I'm so sorry, Kathleen. I'm being rude. This is Brad Kenton, my neighbor. He's been helping me with some repairs to my wheat drill."

"Hello, Brad," Kathleen said, distracted. "What in the world have you two been talking about?"

Judy took a deep breath. "I'm afraid you may have gotten an unpleasant initiation to ranch life." She removed the welding mask from her head. "Do you see the thick smoked lens of this helmet?"

Kathleen took the head gear from Judy and looked through the lens.

"I can't see anything."

"You can't until you start welding. The light is so bright from a welding arc that it can burn your eyes if you look at it for too long without protective lenses."

Kathleen went pale. "My eyes don't feel burned."

"And they may not be. It depends on how closely and how long you looked at the light," Judy said.

"When you wake up to sunlight in the morning is when you'll know," Brad added. "Your eyes will hurt like the dickens if they're burned."

Kathleen turned even whiter. Judy put a supportive hand on her elbow.

"Don't worry, Kathleen. Every welder burns his eyes at some time or another. Even if your eyes are burned, there shouldn't be any permanent damage. You'll just be awful uncomfortable for two or three days, and you'll want to be religious about wearing good sunglasses for the rest of the summer. As a matter of fact, if you've got any with you, I'd wear them now."

Judy and Brad followed as Kathleen walked to the car and retrieved her sunglasses. The city woman's pallor was turning into a hot blush.

"Sorry about the welcome," Judy said.

"I feel like such a fool," Kathleen answered. She pulled her sunglasses from a pocket on the console.

"We're all a little foolish when we go into a new world," Judy said.

"Shoot yeah!" Brad added. "Remember our senior year in high school when we went with 4H to the livestock show in San Antonio?"

Judy laughed. "You, me, Sally Strunk, and Tom Web decided we were all "growed up" and smart enough to figure out the city bus system."

"We ended up in some barrio, instead of at the Alamo."

"Never did figure out how to take the bus back. We finally stopped a cab," Judy recalled.

"By the time we got back to the motel, we were two dollars short of the cab fare."

"You had to leave the driver your pocket knife."

Old laughter bubbled up until Judy and Brad were both fighting a fit of the giggles.

"Good Barlow, too," Brad said.

"Quit complaining. I've given you at least three Barlows for Christmas since then."

"Ain't the same."

The laughter was contagious. Kathleen's embarrassed flush turned to a smile.

"At least you had a sense of humor about it," Kathleen said.

"The hell you say," Brad responded.

Judy's laughter echoed inside the barn. She turned to Kathleen to explain.

"You see, taking the bus was Brad's idea."

"It was nearly a year before Tom would speak to me like I was human. When I asked Sally out two months later, she said 'I prefer to date boys I can depend on.'"

Brad's highpitched imitation of Sally Strunk was the key. A clear, cool spring of laughter bubbled from all three. The dogs wandered back and forth among the humans, caught up in their merriment, and started the barking they'd apparently forgotten at Kathleen's arrival. Weakened from the laughter, Judy leaned against the car and wiped tears from her eyes.

"Now that we've succeeded in burning you and amusing you, I guess we'd better get you settled in," Judy said.

"I take it you're the Kathleen Romero Judy was telling me about," Brad said.

"Sorry, guess I didn't finish introductions," Judy interrupted. "Kathleen, this is Brad Kenton from the next ranch over."

In the image of gallantry, Brad took Kathleen's hand. Judy could have sworn he was going to kiss it.

"Always good to have a new face out here, especially one so pretty," Brad said.

"You'd best put your courting manners away, Brad boy. We've still got work to do," Judy said.

"You sure know how to spoil a man's fun," Brad responded.

Judy turned to Kathleen. "First things first, let's get you settled. Kathleen, why don't you pull up by the house? I guess your bags are in the trunk."

"Yes."

"Brad, how do you feel about being a bell boy?"

The young man smiled devilishly at Kathleen. "Kind of depends on the tip."

"Don't go getting pushy," Judy answered. "You'll get all the bologna sandwiches and corn chips you can eat for lunch."

"That's the same tip I get for being assistant welder."

"Nobody ever said life was fair."

Kathleen laughed. "And I was afraid life in the country would be boring."

Judy smiled. "This is nothing. Wait until Useless has a run-in with a skunk."

Brad and Judy walked the few yards to the house, while Kathleen moved her car. Judy cringed as she watched the nearly new automobile bounce over the rutty caliche of the driveway. After Kathleen opened the trunk, Brad took a suitcase, while Judy grabbed a soft-sided garment bag. Kathleen rushed protectively to take the handles of her camera bag and laptop computer case. They deposited Kathleen's possessions unceremoniously in the front bedroom.

"Iced tea break," Judy announced.

"I'll help," Kathleen said.

"Not on a bet. For today, you're company. You and Brad go sit in the living room."

Kathleen perched on the edge of the couch, while Brad made himself at home. He walked to the window and flipped the switch to turn on the pump to the swamp cooler, hanging outside the window. Kathleen listened, curious to the sound of running water, as the pump carried water to the pads inside the cooler. Brad stood, waiting until he figured the pads were damp and then switched on the fan. Within seconds, cool air was filling the room.

"That feels nice," Kathleen said.

"Evaporative cooling, one of God's gifts to life on the dry plains," Brad answered. He plopped in the recliner, sending the chair into a semireclined position with the smoothness of familiarity.

"Judy tells me you're writing a story about ranch women."

"I started with rural women, but I'm beginning to think that subject is too broad for a single article."

Brad glanced toward the kitchen. He could hear Judy rattling ice cubes and glasses.

"Whatever brings you here, I'm glad. Be nice for Judy to have some company for a while."

"I'm certainly enjoying her. It's not often I feel comfortable with someone this quickly."

Judy entered with three tall glasses on a tray. Each glass was filled to capacity with ice and tea. Each one was sweetened. Judy didn't give her guests a choice. She always figured people who worked on a ranch needed the extra sugar.

Kathleen watched her hostess intently. When Judy looked up to smile, Kathleen shifted her gaze to take in the room and its contents.

"What do you think of my cracker box house?"

"It's nice…comfortable," Kathleen answered.

"You won't think so if you're here for the first Blue Norther of the winter. This part of the house was built about 1905, and there's gaps between the window frame and the walls. You can see the curtains move when there's a really strong wind."

"You said this part of the house?"

"Yes, my grandfather built it. As the family grew and changed, we added on, bit by bit. The latest was in 1960 when the folks added the den and a bedroom."

"I didn't realize your family had been here that long."

"Yes."

"Is that why you stayed?"

"No. I stayed because I love it."

Kathleen's deep, brown eyes looked intently into Judy's. "I'm glad you did."

"Me, too," Judy answered.

"Hey, don't you have any cookies? If I'm going to be an assistant welder and a bellhop, I gotta have more than bologna sandwiches."

Judy laughed. "Chocolate chip do you?"

"Oatmeal would be better."

"You want to make them or drive to town and buy them?"

"Chocolate chip's fine."

Chapter Six

From the kitchen, Judy heard Kathleen's groan as she opened her eyes to the daylight. Of course, Judy had been listening for that groan, expecting it.

The ranch woman paused in the act of making coffee to retrieve a bowl from the cabinet and fill it with ice and water. Judy took a tea towel from the drawer and laid it in the ice water. She knocked on the door of the guest bedroom.

"You okay?" Judy asked.

"No," Kathleen answered.

Judy opened the door and found her guest lying with her right forearm resting protectively over her eyes.

"Hurts like the dickens, don't it?" Judy said.

"That is an understatement."

Judy placed the bowl on the floor beside the bed and wrung the water from the tea towel. After she drained most of the water from the cloth, she folded it into a neat rectangle.

"Try laying this over your eyes," she instructed.

"I don't want to take my arm off my eyes. The light hurts."

Judy sat on the edge of the bed and gently grasped the uncooperative arm by the wrist.

"Scrunch your eyes up. It won't take but an instant, and you'll be amazed what some ice cold water will do."

Kathleen allowed Judy to lift her arm away. The protective arm was barely off Kathleen's eyes before Judy had the ice cold cloth in place.

"God, that feels good," Kathleen said.

"Works great for pinkeye, too."

"Will it...will this hurt my vision?" There was a quaver of fear in Kathleen's voice.

Judy smiled. Without thinking she touched Kathleen's forehead lightly and brushed the hair from her face.

"Not likely, but I am driving you in to see the doctor."

"I thought you had to do something with the tractor and that plow thing today," Kathleen protested, weakly.

"Planting can wait a day. It's not like I've got a million acres of farmland."

"You're very good at taking care of people. I think you missed your calling as a nurse."

"Wrong there. I bet I've doctored more shipping sickness, lump jaw, and pinkeye than any nurse you know."

Kathleen laughed weakly. "I must say, you have a good pastureside manner."

"Just say moo."

"Will a groan suffice?"

"It will if I don't have to put you in the squeeze chute to make you take a pill."

"The what?" Kathleen asked.

"We use a hydraulic chute to hold cattle still while we brand, doctor, and such."

"I need to see this thing."

"Not for a couple of days you don't. All you need

to look at for a while is the inside of your eyelids."

"There go my plans for reviewing my notes from the library."

Judy looked down at her guest. The ranch woman, the loner, was surprised by the tenderness she felt for this woman whom she barely knew.

"I'm going to get you a big glass of orange juice. You need to drink lots of fluids. Do you think you could eat some breakfast?"

"Not on a bet. My head hurts."

"I've got an extra dark pair of sunglasses. You need to wear them any time you don't have something over your eyes. Do you think you can get dressed?"

"I think I can feel my way to the clothes I wore yesterday."

"As soon as you're ready, we'll go to town." Judy glanced at the alarm clock on the nightstand. "By the time we get there, Dr. Stewart's office should be open."

⁂

Kathleen was utterly amazed at the fact that she could get in to see the doctor without an appointment. She had expected a trip to the emergency room.

If the law had allowed, Judy could have saved Kathleen the trouble and expense of visiting the grumpy, old doctor. On the trip to town, Judy told Kathleen that Doc Stewart would prescribe an antibiotic ointment to be placed in the woman's burned eyes, every four hours. He did. Judy would have just used an over-the-counter ointment for herself, but she made sure they filled the prescription variety for Kathleen. Judy also said that he would instruct Kathleen to stay in a darkened room for at least two or three days. He did.

"I'm going to be bored out of my everloving mind," Kathleen said as they stopped in front of the drug store.

"Maybe not. Are you up to staying in the pickup while I go to the library for a few minutes?"

"Judy, you do whatever you need to do while we're in town. I feel like a fool, and I'm so sorry to be causing you so much trouble."

Kathleen felt Judy's intense gaze without looking at her.

"You listen here, Kathleen. You're talking to a country girl. We have a whole different meaning to the word neighbor than city, or even town folk. We live and die by looking out for each other. Right now, you're my neighbor and you're my guest. Whatever kindness I may do you is just paying back a kindness someone else did for me."

Judy didn't give Kathleen time to answer. She threw open the driver's door and slammed it behind her. As Judy entered the drug store, Kathleen's prescription in her hand, Kathleen leaned over to rummage in her purse. Working by touch alone, the writer found her notebook and turned to what she hoped was a blank page. With the messy writing of the temporarily sightless, Kathleen put to paper the truth Judy had just shared.

⚜ ⚜ ⚜

There were cattle to be checked. That didn't stop just because Judy had an injured guest. Once they were home, Judy made Kathleen as comfortable as possible—huge glass of iced tea, more ice water and cold towels, crackers and cheese, etc.— and then left to make her rounds of pastures and wells.

The audio books Judy had checked out from the library saved Kathleen's sanity. All three were written by a man who lived and worked in the Oklahoma Panhandle, not seventy miles from Judy's Texas ranch.

Kathleen had expected the day to be a total loss. Instead, she managed a wealth of research and a few giggles inspired by the ranch humor.

"What are windmill leathers?" Kathleen asked.

Judy stood in the doorway to Kathleen's bedroom, the smell of cattle hanging heavy from her jeans and boots. She took a seat in the wooden rocker that had been her mother's, and pulled off her boots. It was a dry day, as most days are on the High Plains, or the boots would have stayed on the back porch along with the mud they would have carried into the house.

"You use leather seals on the checks at the bottom of windmill well shafts."

"I still don't understand."

"When the windmill pushes the rod down, the checks let the water through so the cylinder will fill above them. When the rod goes up, the checks hold the water so the well casing will fill, then water will flow out the top and into the pipe leading to the stock tank.

"Sounds ingenious."

"They are, until they screw up. It can take a three man crew all day to pull a well and replace the leathers. At least it gives us some use for our old boot tops."

Kathleen looked puzzled behind the sunglasses, still worn despite the darkened room. "You mean you don't buy them already made."

"Yeah, most of the time. But it's not worth a drive to town if you're out. It's easy enough to cut up an old boot and make your own."

Kathleen laughed. "I'm not sure I'd want to drink water pumped up with parts of an old shoe."

"Just adds to the flavor. Besides, one of my neighbors says that, if you won't brush the water bugs to the side to drink out of a stock tank, you're not really thirsty."

Kathleen's face contorted in disgust. "Have you ever done it?"

"I've always been lucky. When I've been caught out without a water jug, the wind's been blowing and I drank the fresh water as it was pumped straight out of the ground."

"Would you drink out of the tank?"

"If I was thirsty enough, I would. The time or two I've been tempted, I just think of my neighbor's sons."

"Why?"

"They've both had amoebic dysentery."

Kathleen laughed. "How do you ranch people do it?"

"Do what?"

Kathleen motioned toward the audio book. "This man can make a hard life sound so funny. You and Brad do it, too."

The chair creaked as Judy rocked a minute before answering. "Our life comes from old, cowboy stock, and there's nothing a cowboy likes better than a good practical joke. I guess we just figure God's got a right to a sense of humor."

Kathleen Romera was a good woman, but she was also a professional. She had the cruel streak present in every heart, and her years as a journalist had taught her that there are times to use cruelty. When working for *The Denver Post,* she'd questioned slippery politicians, rapists, murderers, and unscrupulous businessmen. She didn't like herself when she used it, but she rarely doubted her instincts. They had gotten her many a story and saved her life a time or two. Those instincts took over now.

"Is that what you thought when your parents died…that God had a sense of humor?"

Judy's eyes narrowed. Even muted by the darkened glasses Kathleen wore, the expression made her blood run cold.

"No, that time I just figured he was in need of some good company. You know, folks who wouldn't turn on him for no reason."

Judy picked up her boots and left the bedroom. Kathleen sat in bed and wished her instincts had not chosen that particular moment to be wrong. From the kitchen, she could hear Judy rattling pots and pans as she prepared dinner. Kathleen got out of bed and shrugged into her flannel bathrobe. The light outside had softened to the warm purple of evening, but Kathleen's eyes still ached, sunglasses and all, as she stepped into the relative light of the kitchen.

"You need to go back to a darkened room," Judy said, an edge of steel to her voice.

"It won't hurt me for a few minutes." Kathleen sat at the table and watched as Judy tenderized and breaded round steak. "I'm sorry, Judy. My question was uncalled for. It's just that, well, as a journalist, I sometimes have to take some unfair shots to get people to open up beyond the surface."

Judy turned on her guest. "Do I look like

somebody who lives on the surface?"

Kathleen removed her hand from her injured eyes. She ignored the pain and looked long and hard at Judy.

"No."

"Then why'd you do it?"

Kathleen thought hard as her mind tried to explain, even to herself, why she had asked the hurtful question. It took several moments for an answer to crawl out of the confusion.

"I don't have much time. I guess I was trying to take a short cut to getting to know you."

The steel faded slightly from Judy's face. She turned and started laying chicken fried steaks on the hot skillet. They made a wonderful sound as they sizzled.

"You gotta watch them shortcuts. They can get you in a world of trouble."

"Tell me about it."

Judy glanced over her shoulder. Kathleen's hand was back over her eyes.

"You'd best get back to the dark before your head explodes. We can eat dinner in the living room. It's a lot darker in there."

"Can I help?"

"Ask me that when you're fit again."

Gratefully, Kathleen made her way into the darkened bedroom.

Chapter Seven

They talked for some time, the dirty dinner dishes on the coffee table before them. With childish giddiness, Judy rummaged through her collection of CDs. Kathleen rested her head on the back of the couch, smiling as she realized the joy of Judy sharing her special music. Judy played Faith Hill and classic Waylon Jennings. The steady pulse like beat of country music was a comfortable contrast to the jazz of local bands from Judy's college days. Half way through the evening, Judy returned to the couch with an old album cover in her hand. Judy sat close to her guest, fidgeting nervously as she displayed her autographed copy of *Bob Wills and His Texas Playboys: For the Last Time*. Kathleen removed her sunglasses and looked at the signatures in the subdued light of the darkened living room. Judy pulled out an old turntable and played music that made Kathleen's toes tap and her heart sing, as she studied the handwriting of the men who made the music. Kathleen had heard the term western swing, but before this evening she would have thought the Texas Playboys were a basketball team. She listened with interest, as Judy spoke of Bob Wills and all he had meant to country music.

When Kathleen returned the album cover to its owner, Judy didn't move from her position beside Kathleen. The two women relaxed, their shoulders touching. Kathleen felt the comfort of the ever-so-slight physical contact, but she said nothing and made no move to touch, or mover closer to, her companion.

"I like your music, Judy."

Kathleen didn't open her eyes as Judy raised her head. Without looking, she could feel the warmth of Judy's gaze. Kathleen sat half asleep, her face molded into a peaceful smile.

In the social code of the country, Judy didn't ask about Kathleen's life. Kathleen expected an inquisition. Urban culture expected that questions must be answered, if a person were to be trusted to enter the sanctity of a home. She had her standard safe answers already formed in her mind, but they were never needed. Judy didn't ask.

Kathleen was too comfortable to be surprised, as she heard her own voice. The Chieftains, music that celebrated Judy's own Irish heritage, triggered a memory for Kathleen. She ran her fingers through the soft length of her brown hair, before finally bringing her hands to rest in her lap as the story unfolded.

The words came, softly spoken, the trickle of a tear seeping from closed eyes. She told a simple tale of broken, adolescent dreams, and an old guitar, a gift of sorts from the discards of an aunt. That guitar had been the object of her musical aspirations, as she learned her first crude chords. One day, believing herself alone, she had played and sung with the abandon of the musician she dreamed she would become. The story ended with the cruelty of an older brother, who laughed at her dreams and broke her guitar.

Kathleen sat, unmoving. The music ended, and the two women remained silent.

Judy said nothing, listening intently. For Kathleen, her companion's rapt silence gave her a greater sense of security and safety than any comforting words or physical touch could have done.

"It's getting late," Judy said.

Kathleen squinted despite the subdued light of a single lamp in the next room. "I guess I lost track of time."

"I've got to get to the planting tomorrow morning."

"It's been a relaxing evening. I feel like I could sleep," Kathleen said.

"Take first shot at the bathroom," Judy insisted.

Kathleen rose from the couch, moving slowly from the lethargy of relaxation.

"Kathleen."

"Yes?"

"It's good to have your company."

Kathleen turned to study her hostess.

"The feeling's mutual."

❧ ❧ ❧ ❧

"You still awake?" Judy asked softly from the doorway.

Kathleen was comfortable in the soft, old-fashioned bed, but she was still awake. She had been resting quietly, comforted by the everyday noises of Judy running bath water, and the subtle sounds as the country woman prepared to retire for the night.

"Yeah, I'm still awake."

"If you're up to a midnight excursion, there's something I'd like you to see."

"Sure."

"Get dressed, and I'll meet you in the kitchen. You might want to wear a jacket. It's cool outside." Kathleen could hear excitement in Judy's voice. There was also a tinge of shyness.

Kathleen dressed quickly, not forgetting the jacket Judy had recommended.

"Ready?" Judy asked. Even in the darkness, Kathleen could feel a new timidity from her hostess.

"Ready and willing. What is it you're going to show me?"

Judy laughed nervously. "I hope you don't think it's silly. Ever since I was old enough to go out after dark on my own, I've loved doing this."

"You've got my interest. Now, what is it?"

"I heard them while I was in the bathtub. I thought you might want to pay a visit. Besides, this is something you can see without hurting your eyes."

"Who are we going to visit?"

Judy smiled devilishly. "You'll see."

Neither woman turned on a light, as they prepared for their midnight excursion. There was no adjustment to night vision as they stepped out into the night air. Half a moon stared down at them with its lopsided face. Abruptly, Kathleen turned into a statue of flesh. For a long moment, she did not move as she tried to identify what was different...what was wrong.

"Why's it so...dark?" Kathleen asked.

Judy laughed. "I've heard that question from every city person I've ever brought out here at night. My friend, this is the country. There are no street lights."

Kathleen felt out of sync. She paused to adjust her eyes and her mind to the rural night.

"I've been camping. Why didn't I feel like this?"

"Good question." Judy removed the sweat stained Woorley Mills Feed cap she wore, and toyed with the bill as she thought. "Maybe when you're camping, you take the natural route from day to evening to night. It's gradual. In a country home, you go from the modern environment of the house to the sudden blackness of night."

Kathleen nodded agreement. She was feeling the magic of the night. A deep breath retrieved numerous smells...the pungent scent of horses, a hint of the water reeds growing in the stock pond behind the house. As she gave her mind and soul time to adjust to the night, Kathleen detected the subtle sounds along with the smells. A light breeze rustled the tall grass growing near the house. In the distance, she heard a sporadic yapping.

"What's that?" Kathleen asked.

Judy smiled. "That's what we're going to see."

As Judy answered, the yapping turned to a chorus of howls, some distant, some close, but most centered at a location just over a small hill. The sound gave birth to goose bumps all along Kathleen's arms and legs and, even in the darkness, Judy could see her companion's eyes widen in a combination of excitement and fear.

"You feel it?"

"Jesus, who wouldn't?"

"Now you know why the Indians think of the coyote as magical."

"Will we really see them?"

"If we're careful."

Judy stepped away from the house. She stood with her nose raised to the wind and moved in slow half circles.

"What are you doing?"

"Finding wind direction. We're going to have to walk a ways to come at them from downwind."

"That's okay by me. It's good to be out of the house."

"Do your eyes hurt?" Judy asked.

Kathleen blinked twice. When she concentrated on the sensation, she could still feel a dull ache, but she realized that she had not even thought of her eyes since Judy suggested this adventure.

"No."

"Then let's go."

Kathleen was instructed on the art of breaching a five-wire fence as Judy held one wire down with a foot and others up with her hands. Kathleen crawled through the opening Judy created and then turned to return the favor for Judy. Kathleen laughed quietly, as Judy said that they would need to walk around the hill.

"What's so funny?"

"I'm from Colorado, remember? I don't see anything resembling a hill."

Judy pointed. "See this rise?"

Kathleen looked. "Yes."

"Can you see over it?"

"No."

"That makes it a hill. Now be quiet, and let's get going."

Judy led the way at a quick walk, as they moved to the windward side of a spot the country woman knew well. There was a small arroyo, nearly a mile from the house. When one of the calves in the sick pen died, Judy would drag the carcass to this arroyo to leave as feed for the scavengers. The scattered howling returned to sporadic bits of yapping conversation. All of it came from the arroyo.

Kathleen loved to walk. She had multiple routes through the streets of Colorado Springs that she would walk for hours, nurturing inspiration for when she returned to the computer keyboard. During the harsh Colorado winters, she moved to the hills and mountains and experienced the joys of cross-country skiing. They had walked better than a mile, and Kathleen was disappointed when Judy slowed and glanced toward the crest of the hill.

"Get down," Judy whispered.

They moved at a crouch toward the top of the rise and finished the last few feet at a crawl. The pack was there.

"Damnation," Kathleen whispered and was immediately shushed into silence by Judy.

They silently watched a coyote sitcom. This was Donna Reed, with the three half-grown pups, wasn't quite perennial sweetness. Sure, she made certain the pups got their share of the carcass, but when one adolescent tried to take meat from his mother's mouth he received a nip on the nose. His injured pride—not to mention his nose—sent the pup yapping, with his tail tucked between his legs. For a moment, he lay outside the circle of the group. It didn't last long. One of his siblings romped and played in front of his brother until the injured pup couldn't keep himself from joining the fun. The two finished their game by rolling haphazardly in an ancient carcass, raising a smell that made Kathleen bury her nose in the sleeve of her jacket.

"Why do they do that?" she whispered.

"I've heard that they roll in the remains of their prey to cover their natural odor from future prey."

"I just pray they don't do it again," Kathleen responded.

Judy stifled a laugh. The slight noise caused the

coyote bitch to look up from her meal. She raised her nose to the wind and tested the atmosphere, before returning to the delicacy of steer entrails.

A large male rested half inside the carcass itself, eating whatever he pleased. Periodically, one of the other nine coyotes would slink up to the smorgasbord, snatch a piece of meat or hide, and drag it a safe distance from the growling dominant male.

It was obviously a coyote holiday. The feast brought together the smaller hunting groups of two or three. As they ate, they gathered into those same groups with which they lived and hunted, just as humans would.

Kathleen was starting to feel the cool of the night. Whatever warmth the ground provided, retained from the sun, was rapidly dissipating. The city woman shivered slightly, and Judy reacted immediately.

"Let's go. We've seen enough," she whispered.

They reversed their progress from their approach, crawling and then walking at a crouch. Kathleen warmed almost immediately as they settled into a rapid walk, back toward the house. They walked in silence, each lost in her own thoughts, until they passed, once again, through the five-wire fence.

"Thanks for sharing that with me," Kathleen said as they neared the house.

"Thanks for not thinking it was silly," Judy responded.

Kathleen playfully thumped Judy on the back of the head, knocking the ball cap over Judy's eyes. Kathleen was surprised at her own sense of ease with this stranger.

"Judy?"

"Yeah?"

"Why are you alone?"

Judy pushed the ball cap back from her eyes. Kathleen felt a tad uncomfortable at the intensity of Judy's gaze.

"Who's asking, the reporter or the new friend?"

"The new friend."

"I had somebody once."

"What happened?"

Judy took a deep breath.

"She couldn't handle sharing me with the ranch."

Kathleen turned away, hiding her involuntary smile from her hostess.

"Kathleen."

"Yes?"

"I hope you don't mind sharing a house with a... lesbian. I promise, I'll be a perfect lady."

Kathleen briefly cupped Judy's cheek in her fingers. "I wasn't worried," she said.

Kathleen entered the house and walked straight to her room. It was late, and the fatigue and incongruous events of the day left her feeling headily out of control. She needed sleep.

Judy stood in the moonlight, her hand raised to her own cheek. Eventually, she stumbled into the house, locking the door behind her. She needed sleep, too.

Chapter Eight

It's been a very long time. I'm not sure I remember how," Kathleen said.

Judy smiled devilishly before she answered.

"It's been a long time for me with some things too, but I'm sure they'll come back to me in a heartbeat."

Kathleen chuckled despite her apprehension. She held the reins tentatively, while she stared indecisively at the saddle.

"Are you sure about this?" Kathleen asked.

"I borrowed Old Buck from the neighbors. Their four-year-old son is learning to ride on him."

"Four-year-old you say?"

"And Old Buck's a respectable twenty-two. You'll be a helluva lot safer on him than you are driving on the interstate through Colorado Springs."

"I have one more question."

"What?"

Kathleen took a long, shaky breath. "Do they call him Buck because he likes to?"

"Likes to what?"

"Buck."

Judy laughed so hard she startled Jackson, her gelding, as he stood beside her.

"You really don't know anything about horses, do you?" Judy asked.

"No, why?"

"Old Buck is buckskin colored."

Kathleen looked closely at the gentle gelding. "You mean he's beige?"

Judy laughed again. "Yes, he's beige. Among horsemen, he's called a buckskin." She leaned comfortably against the horse's hind quarters.

"What color is your horse?"

"Jackson's a chestnut sorrel with a bald face."

"His face is white, not bald."

Judy sighed. "Take my word for it. He's called bald-faced in horse talk."

"What other colors are there?"

"That's it! Enough! You're not going to procrastinate another moment. It's time to mount"

"Yeah, right." Kathleen adjusted her sunglasses.

"Your eyes hurt?"

"I wish. If they did, I'd be asking to go inside right now. No, they're all better now."

"Keep the sunglasses on," Judy said.

"The sunglasses stay on my face as long as I can stay on the horse."

"No problem there."

Judy dropped the reins of her well-trained gelding, and took Buck's reins from Kathleen. With the ease of long habit, Judy stepped to a spot just beside the buckskin's left shoulder and placed the reins around his neck. As she held them with one hand, she turned to Kathleen.

"Come on. I'll help you up."

There was a clammy film of sweat on Kathleen's hand as Judy grasped it. Judy squeezed reassuringly.

"I've got a feeling you're going to be a natural."

"Yeah, right."

Old Buck was a small horse. Kathleen was surprised at the ease with which she stepped into the stirrup and lifted into the saddle. Once there, she sat breathlessly looking down on the world. Judy evened the reins and then tied them into a loose knot.

"That wasn't so bad, was it?" Judy asked.

"Ask me that after we start moving."

Judy turned to her own horse and quickly mounted, despite the brief dance step Jackson attempted as she stepped into the stirrup.

"Let's go," Judy said

At an easy pace, Judy led the way toward the gate to the pasture behind the house.

"What do I do?" Kathleen called.

"Think forward and let your body tell Old Buck what to do."

Kathleen tried it. Much to her surprise, the instructions worked.

❧❧❧❧

Judy was right. Kathleen took to horses like a natural. Before they finished that first ride, the city woman and Old Buck achieved a comfortable understanding. Old and gentle as he was, every horse has a point at which they test their rider. The moment came as they neared the north edge of the back pasture. The two women were riding at a slow walk, when Old Buck suddenly stopped, lowered his head to the ground, and began happily munching on fresh, green shoots of grass growing under the protective cover of the longer, ripened blades.

The expert kept her advice to herself and gently pulled Jackson to a stop. She leaned back, her hand on the cantle of the saddle, and sat patiently waiting.

Kathleen thought *head up* and *forward*, and her

hand pulled naturally at the reins, while her heels kicked lightly at Old Buck's sides. The buckskin continued happily munching.

"I'm thinking the right thoughts, but he isn't listening," Kathleen said.

"You're being tested," Judy responded.

"Great." A wave of red, matching the highlights of her dark brown hair, crept up Kathleen's face.

"You getting pissed off?" Judy asked.

"Yes."

"Good. Let him know."

With the added energy of anger, Kathleen thought *head up* and *forward*. Her hand jerked more viciously at the reins, and her heels dug deep into Old Buck's side.

Unsurprised, Old Buck jerked his head up and progressed immediately into a slow trot. Instinctively, Kathleen's hand pulled at the reins, using just the right amount of pressure to slow Buck to a walk.

Judy's grin nearly split her face, as she rode to a spot beside Kathleen.

"What are you smiling at?" Kathleen asked, a slight edge of anger still in her voice.

"You're going to do fine, just fine," Judy said.

That was Kathleen's first day on a horse. It was not her last. Before the day was out, she was loping comfortably beside Judy. Before the week was out, she had ceased needing the nightly hot baths to soak away her soreness. Before two weeks ended, she was converted from a tenderfoot to an active helper, as Judy worked cattle and rode fences.

The saddlebags filled with medicine bottles, syringes, and colored chalk were transferred from Judy's saddle to Kathleen's. Judy used the chalk to mark the faces of the steers each day they were doctored. She used red one day, yellow the next, and orange the third. If a steer's face held three marks, he was brought into the sick pen where he received additional feed and attention.

When a sick animal was spotted, Judy and Jackson worked together to rope the steer, then Kathleen would lope to her side. The two women would wrestle the animal to the ground, at the same time shooing away the unwanted assistance of Useless and Somegood. Kathleen learned, with ease, the art of kneeling on the animal's shoulder to keep him pinned to the ground, while Judy applied medicine and gave him the appropriate chalk mark. Once the animal was released, they would resume their ride through the pasture, searching for sick animals. There weren't many. Judy preferred to buy crossbred Hereford and Longhorns, a cross noted for high natural resistance to disease.

Once Judy realized that Kathleen actually intended to work, she made a brazen raid on her absent brother's closet. Kathleen's designer jeans were neatly folded in her suitcase, where they were likely to stay throughout the duration of her visit. The borrowed jeans were slightly big, but rolled-up cuffs and a good, strong belt solved that problem. Judy's jeans would have fit Kathleen if she weren't a good four inches taller than her hostess. As it was, Judy was very pleased at how Kathleen looked in her borrowed work shirts.

"This is a helluva lot easier since you came to visit," Judy said as they loaded the horses into the trailer. They had just finished checking the last pasture.

"I never thought of doing work like this, and I can't believe how much I enjoy it."

"Will it help your story?"

"God, yes. Even if I had interviewed country women from now until Christmas, I couldn't have gained the insight I'm getting by working with you."

"Good. I'd feel guilty if you weren't getting anything out of it."

For a moment, Kathleen looked at Judy with an unexpected vulnerability in her eyes. Judy stared into those eyes, but no sooner than she noted the unexpected expression, it was gone.

"Let's get back to the house. I'm hungry," Kathleen said.

Judy started the pickup. "I'd say this would be a good night to crank up the grill and broil a couple of T-bones."

As if on cue, Kathleen's stomach growled and both women laughed.

"Don't talk about it. Let's do it."

Judy wrestled the gear stick into *Granny* so that the well-used ranch pickup could pull the trailer and horses up a slight incline. They rattled and banged across the pasture until they came to the gate. Kathleen jumped out of the pickup, lowered the gate to the ground, and waited, while Judy drove over the wire and onto the entrance to the county road.

"You sure you weren't born to the country in another life?" Judy asked as Kathleen jumped back into the pickup, the newly secured gate standing behind them.

"I swear, before coming here, I was a complete city girl. I've always enjoyed hiking and camping, but I never had a chance to really live in the country."

"You sure do take to it."

"I love it. I'll be sad when this assignment is

over."

A lead weight pulled at Judy's heart. She hid her feelings by turning her full attention to the routine tasks of shifting gears and pulling onto the road. Judy didn't like to think about losing the comforting presence of Kathleen.

Judy drove a little faster than she usually did on the rutted county road with a trailer behind her. In the mirror, she could see Jackson and Buck with their legs spread, balancing against the rough ride. They didn't seem to mind. The horses were also looking forward to the comfort of home.

"I wonder who that is," Judy asked as she pointed into the distance. A second vehicle, driving toward the two women, was raising a prestigious cloud of dust. As it drew closer, Judy spotted the blue tones of Brad Kenton's stepside Chevrolet. Judy slowed and eased to one side of the road, while Brad did the same from the opposite direction. They both stopped, side by side, and leaned through the open windows. In an instant, Useless and Somegood jumped out of the back of Judy's pickup, while Brad's dog, Hank, did the same from his master's vehicle. The three dogs marauded the area in a frenzy of peeing on tires and smelling at tails.

"Haven't seen much of you two ladies," Brad said.

"Been busy," Judy answered.

Brad pointedly looked past Judy. "Kathleen, you must be pretty good help. Judy hasn't called me once to help her fencing or checking cattle, since the doctor pronounced you fit."

"I love it," Kathleen answered, half yelling to make herself heard outside the pickup cab.

Brad stopped the motor of his pickup and

stepped out. He walked past Judy and around the front of her pickup to lean on Kathleen's door. With open curiosity, Brad peered closely at Kathleen.

"Judy girl, I've seen this shirt before, but it don't look quite the same."

"Each horse wears his saddle a different way," Judy answered.

"Yeah," Brad grinned devilishly. "And some better than others."

"Careful, boy. You may end up with a burr under this saddle," Judy said. There was a hint of tension to her smile.

Kathleen blushed.

"Don't mean to be rude, Miss Kathleen. It's just that it always does a country boy's heart good to see a woman who can fit in with ranching life and still look like a woman."

"What am I, chopped liver?" Judy asked.

"Did I say I was just talking about Kathleen? Lord, woman, you should know by now what I think of you."

Judy shook her head and forced a laugh.

"Where you been, anyway?" she asked.

"Dad's pickup blew a fuel line. I've been to town for parts."

"Hear any good gossip?"

"Nothing new. Somebody's supposed to have caught the mayor working after hours with his secretary. You know that nice couch in his office?"

"Yeah, real leather."

"First I'd ever heard that it folds out into a bed."

Judy turned to Kathleen. "Don't you just love small-town gossip?"

"Anybody pay any attention to it?" Kathleen

asked.

"A few of the holier than thou folks. Most of us just consider it a source of entertainment."

"That's interesting."

Brad left his perch against the pickup and shuffled toward his own vehicle. "I'd best get going. Dad's going to be fit to tied. He feels like he's crippled when his pickup's down."

"See you, neighbor," Judy called. Kathleen waved, halfheartedly.

Once the two women and their entourage of animals were bouncing down the road again, Kathleen turned to Judy.

"There's something I think you should tell your friend."

"What's that?"

"He's not my type."

She knew it was unwarranted, but Judy felt the lead weight fall from her heart.

"I'll get word to him, but that's not likely to stop good, old Brad."

"I'll tell him if he gets too pushy."

Judy glanced toward her companion.

"What is your type?"

Kathleen blushed.

"Haven't you guessed?"

Judy felt her mouth go dry. "I'm a little dense some times."

Kathleen studied the other woman long and hard. "No, Judy, you're not dense. You're just too damn polite sometimes."

Judy licked her lips, trying to will moisture back to her mouth. "I'll have to see if I can do something about that."

Chapter Nine

Relax, will you? You look scared half to death," Judy said as she shifted gears.

Kathleen sat with an asparagus casserole balanced carefully in her lap. Both women were freshly washed, their hair shining, and Kathleen was, once again, wearing her designer jeans. Still, the woman had not completely reverted to her city ways. Not a hint of makeup covered her face. Judy was also without makeup, but then, Judy was always without makeup.

"So it shows?" Kathleen asked.

"You look as nervous as steer invited to a barbecue."

"It's just that this is a whole new world. I've never been to a—what do you call it?"

"A community meeting."

"I've never been to a community meeting before."

Judy glanced at her companion sympathetically. "You've already met most of these people."

"Yes, but not in a social setting."

Judy barked an uncontrollable laugh. "A social setting? Lord, woman, these are just plain, old country folks, not high society."

There was a hint of hurt in the brown of Kathleen's eyes. Judy regretted her laughter.

"I'm sorry," Judy said. "What is it they say? Familiarity breeds contempt. I guess it's just hard for me to imagine the friends and neighbors I've known all my life being particularly intimidating."

Moving carefully, still balancing the casserole as Judy drove, Kathleen turned to face her companion.

"You don't really care what people think or whether or not they accept you, do you?"

Judy's eyes narrowed. "I don't suppose I thought about it much."

"That's what I mean. If you worried what people thought, you'd think about it."

A slow smile teased at Judy's face. "I care what some people think. That's what's so tough about loving folks. I care and then I can get hurt."

Kathleen sighed. "God, I wish I could feel like that."

Judy pulled the pickup off the road and pulled into a makeshift parking place. Her pickup joined the rows of other work-battered vehicles parked outside a retired one-room school house. No classes had been held there for six decades, but the structure maintained its right to exist by serving as a community building for a rural area covering forty square miles.

As Kathleen reached for the door handle, Judy placed a hand on her shoulder, causing Kathleen to hold her place on the pickup seat.

"We don't have to go," Judy said. "You're my guest and my friend. I don't want to force you into a situation you find uncomfortable."

Kathleen laughed. "I'm just nervous, not paralyzed. Don't forget, I've never been to anything like this. I don't know all the social rules."

"The rules are simple," Judy said as she smiled. "Have a good time and try not to piss anybody off. If you can't do both, just worry about having a good time."

They were both laughing as they walked from the pickup, Kathleen carrying the casserole, and Judy the peach pie that had ridden on the seat between them. Kathleen took a deep breath as Judy opened the door and the sounds of voices and laughter came out to greet them.

"Here we go," Kathleen said.

Once again, Judy was right.

Never in her life had Kathleen been in a social setting where people were so intent on making a newcomer comfortable. She assumed the kindness she had seen in Judy and the Kentons had been a part of their individual personalities. She was beginning to realize that country hospitality was not a myth. It was reality.

Shannon Harris showed infinite patience with Kathleen, as he turned over his hand of "42" and stood over her shoulder, guiding her in the subtleties of the game. Occasionally, he'd reach down with a work-calloused hand and point delicately at a domino, helping her play.

"I didn't know dominoes could be so complicated," Kathleen said.

"This ain't dominoes," old Bo Smith said, a tidbit of pie crust escaping his dentures as he spoke. "Dominoes is for children. This here's a sophisticated game."

"Took me forty years to learn it right," Melba Smith said as she stared at the dominoes, passed her wrinkled face. "Every time I think I got it right, this old fart (she pointed at Bo) up and figures out a new twist."

"We wouldn't want our marriage to get boring now, would we dear?" Bo responded as he deftly took another trick.

"Damn," Melba said.

"Now, honey. That ain't no way to talk like a lady," Bo said.

"So I'm a lady, am I? I'll remember that next time you need help hauling posts."

"This little lady's proving to be quite a hand," Brad said. Kathleen hadn't noticed his approach, but she now felt his presence, all to close, at a spot just behind her.

"So I heard," Mable responded. "It's about time Judy got some help on that place. Whatever made you decide to work as a farm hand?"

"Actually, I'm just visiting, while I do some research," Kathleen answered.

"Yeah, Kathleen's a writer," Brad said. Kathleen was finding his presence irritating.

"Lord-a-mercy, Brad Kenton! Why don't you go cut another slice of pie and let the woman talk for herself? If she can write, I imagine she can talk," Mable said.

Mable was not known for her patience. Most folks didn't mind. She was known for her loving kindness to one and all. The old woman was just a little gruff at how she expressed it.

"You don't fool me, Mable. You just want me to bring you another slice of the coconut cream," Brad said.

"Well, since you're up..." Mable answered.

Brad turned to the kitchen, located in one end of

the former classroom.

It didn't take Kathleen long to decide that she was out of her league at the "42" table. She quickly returned her seat to Shannon and proceeded to drift to another table. Each table had its own personality, and Kathleen made a point of visiting each one, her misgivings long forgotten. She saved Judy's table for last, because she knew that was where she would stay. Although they went nearly two hours without speaking to one another, Kathleen was comforted by Judy's subtle attention. Like a child looking for her mother, Kathleen caught herself glancing frequently in Judy's direction. Every time she looked, there was momentary eye contact. Judy was watching her, anxious and protective. Kathleen had no doubt that, if anyone did anything to make her uncomfortable, Judy would be by her side in an instant.

At one table, recipes had flown like birds in spring. The new farm program was being carefully dissected at another, and tales of childbirth had sent Kathleen rapidly scurrying past a third. Through it all, a small herd of children, ages two to twelve, weaved in and out the tables and in and out the front door, in a series of obscure games understood only by the children.

Everywhere she had been, people had paused to ask how she liked the country and if she was enjoying the stay. What amazed Kathleen was not their questions, but that the people really seemed to care about her answers.

Kathleen had nearly finished her rounds and was approaching the empty chair waiting expectantly beside Judy.

"You folks are just too darned quiet," Brad called.

He rose from where he was leaning against the back of a chair, halfheartedly listening to the conversation at the nearest table. He walked quickly, his boots making a distinctive clomp, clomp on the wooden floor, toward the elderly stereo resting near the door.

"I'd say it's time to dance," Brad said as he pulled an old-style album from its protective cover and placed it on the stereo.

Mabel cackled. "I was beginning to worry about you young folks. When we were your age, Brad, Bo here would have had his fiddle out an hour ago."

A kindly woman, one whose name had escaped Kathleen in the frenzy of introductions, turned to explain. "Bo's arthritis got too bad about ten years ago. We haven't had a fiddler since. Have to settle for records and such."

Kathleen was saved from an answer by the eruption of Bob Wills and the Texas Playboys. Bo and Mable were on the floor before the first fiddle note had ended, and Kathleen heard Judy whoop from across the room. Judy did a fancy little shuffle as she crossed the floor, meeting Brad half way. In moves speaking of practice and familiarity, Brad and Judy were soon dancing in synchronized rhythm in a pattern both strong and graceful. Kathleen had not seen country-western dancing before. She thought it a nice combination of ballroom precision and modern rhythm. It looked like fun.

Those who weren't dancing were moving tables and chairs to open up the dance floor. Kathleen joined the scuffle and scrap of the group as she grabbed two chairs and carried them to the side. Brad led Judy in a neat circle and twirled his dancing companion to a neat halt at a spot just beside Kathleen.

"Your turn," Brad said as he held his hand out for Kathleen.

"No way. I've never done this before."

"It's easy. Judy and I been dancing the two-step since we were kids," Brad said.

"That's why it's easy for you. If you don't mind, I'll pass."

"It really is fun, Kathleen. Nobody here will care if you do it right," Judy said, a flush of pleasure on her face.

Reluctantly, Kathleen took Brad's hand.

"You look awful pretty," Brad said, just as Kathleen missed the motion and placed her right toes squarely under his boot.

"Ouch! Please talk less and try to help me do this."

"It's easy. Just follow me."

Brad moved in an exaggerated version of the two-step. For a moment, it seemed Kathleen may have grasped the motion, when their right feet collided painfully, and Kathleen pushed Brad away not too gently.

"That's it. Enough!" Kathleen said. "I can't dance to anything where you actually have to know the steps."

Brad tried to take her right hand and place his right hand on her waist. "Come on. You just need a little practice."

"I can't stand the bruises," Kathleen answered, backing away.

"One round of the floor, and you'll get the feel." Brad moved closer.

Judy inched between them. "She doesn't want to dance, Brad boy. Give her some room."

"Jealous?" Brad asked.

Judy's smile almost hid the spark of anger in her eye. "Yes."

"In that case, I guess I'll have to dance with you."

The couple whirled away, at least as much as they could whirl on the now crowded dance floor. Despite their gaiety, something was missing. The air of companionship apparent in their earlier dance was gone.

❧ ❧ ❧ ❧

"That wasn't so bad, was it?" Judy asked as they stepped from the back porch and into the kitchen.

"I had a blast."

"Brad didn't bother you too much, did he?"

"No, not really, although I was glad you were there to save me from the two-step."

Judy placed the empty casserole dish and pie plate in the sink and filled them with water.

"I still think you'd enjoy country-western dancing if you had a chance to learn."

"Not with a roomful of people watching and Brad making me feel like a klutz by telling me how easy it is."

Judy laughed. "The man can be a bit pushy at times. Actually, once you get comfortable with the pattern, it is easy. It just takes a little while to train your legs the new way of moving."

"Would you teach me?"

A flush of pleasure covered Judy's face. She tried to hide it by turning to the sink and repositioning the pans.

"Sure. Wait here."

Judy crossed to the stereo in the living room. In a moment, a soft country tune flowed through the house. It was slower, easier than the Bob Wills and Reba McEntire music Brad had played at the community building. Kathleen didn't recognize the band, but she liked it.

"Help me move these," Judy said as she returned to the kitchen and pushed the table and chairs against the wall.

"I didn't mean for you to go to so much trouble. I—"

"Now watch."

Slowly, Judy went through the step, step-shuffle-step; step, step-shuffle-step of the two-step.

"Stand beside me," Judy commanded.

Kathleen followed her instructions. Moving in tandem and slowly, Kathleen duplicated Judy's movements. In a very short time, she had settled into the rhythm.

"I'll lead," Judy said as she stepped in front of Kathleen.

It seemed to Kathleen that they moved magically together, almost from the first.

"You act like you've done this before," Kathleen said.

Kathleen could feel the heat of Judy's embarrassed blush. "Yes, I've taught other women to dance the two-step."

"Did any of them learn this quickly?"

Judy looked up. Kathleen caught the full view of Judy's ice blue eyes. For a moment, the woman felt hypnotized by the color.

"No, none of them learned this quickly."

The music drifted to a close, and a new tune began.

"Can we dance to this?" Kathleen asked, not wanting the moment to end.

"This is a waltz. It's a little different."

"Show me."

In answer, Judy grasped Kathleen's hand tightly and placed her arm snugly around the other woman's waist.

"The cowboy waltz is just a skating step. If Brad were here, he'd say it was easy, and he'd be right. Just move with me."

Kathleen did just that. She moved with and closer to Judy. They fell into an empathetic rhythm, and without being truly taught the cowboy waltz, Kathleen was dancing. Her body seemed to read Judy's before the country woman even moved.

The magic was there. They both could feel it like a perfume in the air. Without permission, Kathleen's hand moved from Judy's shoulder to her hair and finally to a gentle caress of Judy's cheek. The blue of Judy's eyes, as she stared unwavering at Kathleen's face, intensified to the deep shade of an early evening sky.

When the song ended, they did not move apart.

Kathleen leaned close and moved her hand up Judy's shoulder and neck until it rested firmly on the back of her head. Judy didn't resist as Kathleen gently positioned her head so that Judy's lips neared Kathleen's. As the next tune began, they kissed. Neither woman heard the music nor saw the harsh white of the utilitarian kitchen light. Kathleen made sure that Judy felt nothing but the softness of her lips and the warmth of her open mouth.

All in all, it was an incredible end to a very pleasant evening.

Chapter Ten

For the most part, the cups rested untouched on the table, their contents growing tepid and then cold. Judy made the coffee (decaffeinated because of the late hour) more out of a need for something to do than from any real desire for the beverage.

Their first kiss ended naturally, breathlessly, followed by a long moment of awkward awareness, as each woman searched for the other's reaction, while trying to hide her own. It was one of those rare moments of vulnerability when humans briefly know what it's like for a cat caught in a refrigerator full of tuna. Both women had found something they wanted, but the future was uncertain.

Judy turned to making coffee and, without a word, Kathleen gathered cups, sugar bowl, and milk jug, and collected them all on a tray. They'd done it all before. This was not the first evening Judy and Kathleen spent visiting over coffee. When it was made and poured, they took their customary seats on the couch. They sat close, neither asking but agreeing, and Judy's hand reached to grasp Kathleen's softer fingers in her own. Using her free hand, Kathleen poured coffee.

"You did know about me, didn't you?" Kathleen asked.

"Know what?"

Kathleen looked at Judy, puzzled.

"I need you to say it," Judy said. "I need to know that you are comfortable with that part of yourself.

"That I'm gay," Kathleen said, a crooked smile hiding her embarrassment.

"I'd hoped," Judy answered.

Judy raised Kathleen's hand to her lips and lightly kissed the fingers. Kathleen moved closer, and their arms found new niches around each other's bodies. This kiss was longer, less uncertain. Finally, with a sigh, Kathleen moved so that their lips separated, and she rested her head comfortably on Judy's shoulder. Judy lounged fully against the couch, the picture of pleasure and comfort.

"You do that well," Judy said.

"So do you."

"I've wanted to long enough."

"Really," Kathleen said, leaning back to look for truth in Judy's eyes.

"Really," Judy responded, answering even more convincingly with her lips.

This time, it was Judy who pulled away.

"Talk to me," Judy said.

"I was enjoying the nonverbal communication."

"Me, too, but my head's spinning."

"What do you want to know?"

"Is there anybody else, maybe back in Colorado Springs?" Judy asked. She held her breath, waiting for the answer.

"Not anymore. Laura moved out about a year ago."

"How long had you been together?"

"Four years," Kathleen answered.

Judy said nothing. Her face was open and curious, but she wouldn't ask. The country woman felt that Kathleen would tell her what she wanted her to know. She did.

"When I started freelancing full-time, Laura couldn't handle the insecurity." There was a note of bitterness in Kathleen's voice. "She left me for a man."

"If it was security she wanted, she went to the right place. Most men are raised to provide security and demand ownership."

"No shit."

Judy laughed. "I take it you talk from experience."

"I tried the straight thing for a while. Nearly got married once, but sanity returned in time," Kathleen said.

"Men aren't that bad," Judy countered.

Kathleen ran her fingertips over Judy's face. "So, I understand that I'm not the first woman you've kissed."

"No, you're not." It was Judy's turn for pain in her voice. "I was with Sandy for nearly six years."

"Could you possibly live with a man after knowing what it's like to love a woman?"

They kissed before Judy answered.

"No," she said. Kathleen already knew the answer.

"Tell me about Sandy."

Judy closed her eyes and allowed herself to be carried on a flood of memory.

"God, she was wonderful!"

A hint of fear crossed Kathleen's face. "You still love her."

"Her or maybe just her memory. It's long over between us. I haven't heard from her in months, and the last time I called, it was obvious she felt nothing. She was polite." Judy made the word sound like an unwanted itch.

"What happened between you?" Kathleen asked.

"She couldn't understand my need to come back here."

"God, this is a beautiful life."

"Sandy thought so, too, for two to three week intervals. In the end, I came back here, and she stayed in the city."

"What made you decide to come back?"

Judy's mind was trying to form an answer when something happened, something she had not anticipated. The words she sought mixed with feelings long ignored. The tears flowed.

"Good Lord. What's wrong with me?" Judy said as she swiped at her eyes with her bare arm.

Kathleen wrapped her arms around Judy and kissed the tears from her cheeks.

"Old pain, babe," Kathleen said. "We've all got some. Feel now. Talk later."

The offered warmth was too much for the last of Judy's self-control. She was soon sobbing in Kathleen's arms, mumbling erratically about the deaths of her parents and the secret betrayal she still felt at them leaving her alone. Their untimely accident forced Judy into the choice between returning to the ranch or losing the life and the home that had been her anchor for as long as she could remember.

The tears were finally spent. Judy quivered in exhaustion, her head cradled between Kathleen's breasts. At the back of her mind she knew of the sodden mess she was making on Kathleen's blouse, but the arms held her tight and Judy didn't have the will to leave.

"Feel better?" Kathleen asked.

With a shaky breath, Judy sat upright. She paused to test the state of her own feelings. She was surprised at what she found. Her heart felt light.

"Yes," Judy said.

"Is the coffee still hot?

"Should be." Judy started to rise. "I'll get..."

"Sit. I'll get it."

"But you're company."

"Not anymore, babe."

A shaky laugh was Judy's only answer.

They sat in silence, sipping the fresh coffee.

"You must be exhausted," Kathleen said as she gently stroked Judy's arm.

"Yes."

"Maybe we should go to bed," Kathleen said, her voice an expectant whisper.

Judy sat thinking. She paused for a long moment until she finally reached a decision.

"My daddy usually gave good advice."

"Such as?"

"He always said that, with love, you needed to give yourself time to see if it was your body or your heart doing the talking."

"Meaning?"

Judy took Kathleen's face between her hands and kissed her slowly. When Kathleen whispered a soft moan, Judy pushed her away gently.

"Meaning, goodnight Kathleen. I'll see you in the morning." Judy rose from the couch and walked shakily toward her own bedroom.

"Judy," Kathleen called, shocked.

Judy turned to face her.

"There's time, Kathleen. It's better when you take your time."

Kathleen waved her hands absently, trying to understand.

"Yeah, I guess so. Goodnight, Judy."

"Goodnight…and Kathleen…"

"Yes?"

"Thanks."

Kathleen smiled in answer.

❧ ❧ ❧ ❧

Useless was asleep, but her nose was still alert. It was always alert. Even if she was dead and buried, the smell of a fresh steak bone could probably revive the dog.

A scent yanked her awake as she slept in a huddle next to Somegood underneath the porch of the house. Useless woofed twice, loud enough to awaken her sleeping companion, but not loud enough to rouse the woman who was head of their pack. Useless jumped to her feet as Somegood stretched and moaned.

Useless trotted toward the barn, stopping a few feet away from the house and looking expectantly back at Somegood. The border collie rose reluctantly, making a noise dangerously close to a growl as she stood. The two dogs began the familiar walk to the other den in their territory.

The smell became stronger as they drew close. Even Somegood was now awake and sniffing. Useless led the way to the source of the smell. The two dogs went directly to the stalls beside the corrals, following a sweet scent of horse, blood, sweat and something else…something Useless couldn't quite remember.

Sally Doc Bar stood tensed in the stall. Useless walked to the back side of the mare and lifted her nose. Now that she was close, Useless identified the smell and remembered. There was a newborn on the way and soon.

The mare neighed helplessly, and both dogs whined in sympathy. Sally was part of their pack. They were there to help and protect.

White showed around the edge of Sally Doc Bar's eyes and her muscles quivered from the tension. Useless barked halfheartedly a couple of times as she considered the possibility of creating enough noise to bring Judy's welcome presence. Relying on instinct, the dog grew silent. Her nose and heart, if not her mind, told her that Judy was not needed.

Somegood approached the mare. The dog raised her nose as the mare lowered hers. The two animals touched noses in an expression of comfort common to both species. Sally relaxed somewhat in the company of the two dogs. Moving in a tight circle, the mare finally lowered herself to the hay. The two dogs gathered near her and lay against the horse, offering their warmth. There was nothing to do but wait.

Useless dozed, but her nose remained alert. It was always alert.

Chapter Eleven

Y ou awake?" Judy asked. She sat on the edge of Kathleen's bed with one hand gently caressing the city woman's cheek.

Kathleen stretched and yawned. "No."

"Then wake up, there's something I want you to see."

Judy gave Kathleen a light kiss on the lips. Kathleen grasped the back of Judy's head and held her close, prolonging the kiss. Judy didn't seem to mind.

"Will you come in with me?" Kathleen asked, lightly raising the edge of the covers.

Judy smiled. "I already have on my work clothes and boots."

"I don't care."

"There's cow shit on the boots."

Kathleen's eyes opened a little wider. "Okay, I mind, but you could take them off."

"Darlin', you'll really want to see this," Judy said. Kathleen was now awake enough to sense the excitement in Judy's voice.

"See what?"

"I'm not telling. You'll have to get dressed and see it with your own eyes."

"This bed is nice and warm, and you're cruel."

In one swift movement, Judy yanked back the covers, fully exposing Kathleen to the mild chill of the spring morning.

"Damn you!" Kathleen yelled, amused and irritated.

Judy had not anticipated her own reaction to her impulsive behavior. Her gaze was locked on the sight of Kathleen, dressed only in a flimsy nightshirt, the shape of her breasts, nipples erect from the sudden change in temperature, clearly visible beneath the thin cloth. Hungry for more, Judy's gaze drifted down Kathleen's firm body, past the slightly rounded hips and onto the curvy runner's legs of the naturally athletic woman. The smoothness of Kathleen's skin on thigh and calf drew Judy's hand like a magnet. Judy felt her resolve to wait melting like butter in a hot pan. Kathleen inhaled sharply, and Judy looked into the other woman's eyes. She saw there a reflection of her own passion.

"I'll pour coffee," Judy said, her voice husky. She then turned to leave the room in a graceless retreat.

For a moment, Kathleen sat in frustrated silence. When the inertia left her, it took less than a minute for her to don her clothes and walk into the kitchen where she could hear Judy rattling cups and pouring coffee.

"Why did you do that?" Kathleen asked. She stood just inside the kitchen, her long hair in an uncombed rumple.

Judy stood facing the counter. She said nothing.

"We both already know we're gay, so there's no big trauma there; the attraction between us is obvious." There was a hint of anger in Kathleen's voice. "I want to know why you ran away last night and again this morning."

Judy did not turn.

"I've only had three lovers, two really."

Kathleen's voice was a whisper. "I'd like to be

number four."

Judy turned then. There was longing in the blue of her eyes. "I'd like that, too."

"Then let it happen."

Judy picked up both coffee cups and crossed to the table where she sat. She placed one cup in front of her and the second at the seat she obviously intended for Kathleen. She read the signal and sat.

"There's something you should know."

"Jesus, don't tell me you've got AIDS."

Judy laughed. "Nothing quite that drastic."

"Herpes?"

"Good Lord, no! It's just that..."

"Go on."

Judy looked deeply into Kathleen's eyes, searching for understanding.

"Like it or not, whether I want to or not, I can't sleep with anyone without giving her a little piece of my soul."

Kathleen touched Judy's hand, offering understanding and comfort. "I could have guessed that of you, without you telling me."

"It makes me cautious, Kathleen. Before I make love to a woman, I have to know I'm in love with her because God knows I will be after."

A twinge of fear crossed Kathleen's face, followed by a rapid-fire series of emotions that flashed across her features too quickly to be read.

"God, I've scared you away," Judy said, pain taking the breath from her lungs.

"No." Kathleen said, her hand suddenly holding Judy's firmly. "I've just...I just haven't been quite as conscientious as you have. I've not always thought through the consequences of my actions before making them reality." Kathleen took a long drink of her coffee. Her hand was shaking slightly. "Judy, can't you see that I'm already half in love with you?"

"I'd hoped so," Judy said as she stared into the mystery of her plain, black coffee as it rippled in the cup.

"That doesn't frighten me. I just feel good about that, but now, as you talked, I realized that you…that you may grow to care deeply for me. God, Judy, that's terrifying."

"Why?"

"Because you're one of the good people, Judy Proctor. You're one of God's masterpieces, one who should be cherished and nurtured."

"I'm no masterpiece. I'm just a country girl."

"A country girl who's taught me to feel oneness with nature, to see and feel beyond the limitations of my own skin."

Judy held Kathleen's hand between her own.

"Then we'll give it time," Judy said.

"Yeah, we'll give it time."

Judy's chair scraped against the floor as she stood. "Get your boots on. I'll bust if you don't come see this with me soon."

"What about breakfast?"

"Later."

Kathleen's laugh eased the last of the tension hanging in the air. "Okay, let's go."

It didn't take long for Kathleen to finish getting ready, despite the morning trip to the bathroom that she had delayed longer than comfort dictated. Judy waited impatiently on the porch, holding a thermos about which Kathleen wondered but didn't bother to ask. Judy led the way across the farmyard at a walk, verging on a trot.

"What's the hurry?" Kathleen asked.

"You'll see," Judy answered.

Useless and Somegood met them half way across the yard, and both dogs seemed as excited as their mistress. As the women climbed the corral fence, not bothering with the nearby gate, Kathleen saw the cause of all the excitement, and her heart picked up its beat in a joy she now shared with the others.

The newborn filly wobbled and walked in the enclosed perimeters of the stall, still exploring her new world. Sally Doc Bar stood patiently when the filly completed her brief exploration and then wobbled back to nibble and push at every spot where one of her mother's legs joined body until she finally struck upon the right combination. The newborn latched onto a teat like she was holding on for dear life and sucked at her mother.

"That may be the most beautiful sight I've ever seen in my life," Kathleen said.

"I told you, you'd want to see."

"Okay, you were right." Kathleen watched, entranced, as the filly continued her meal. "Is it a boy or a girl?" Kathleen asked.

"It's a filly."

Kathleen looked askew at Judy. "Put that in city language, please."

"It's a girl."

"Can I pet her?"

Judy closed one eye as she assessed the situation. "Give the mare a little time to adjust. We'll ask her real nice, later in the day, if she minds if we play with her baby."

"I hope she lets us."

"Me, too. If you handle them when they're young, they're much easier to break when they're older."

"Gee, I just want to pet her because she's cute and playful."

Judy laughed and then raised the thermos full of hot water. "If you want to stay and watch for a while, I'm going to fix a warm bran mash for Miss Sally. She's had a tough night."

"Judy," Kathleen called as the other woman walked away.

"What?"

Kathleen didn't let her gaze flicker from the sight of mare and colt. "Thanks for waking me."

"Anytime."

Judy turned and walked toward the feed shed. She would make the new mother a hot breakfast, a treat the mare knew only as a part of the joy of giving birth. It was Judy's own way of saying thank you.

❧ ❧ ❧ ❧

A full breakfast of bacon, eggs, fried tomatoes, and biscuits was half consumed when the jangle of the phone interrupted their meal. Judy chewed twice and swallowed to rid herself of the last mouthful before she answered the phone.

"Hello," she said. There was a pause. "Sure, I'll help." Another pause. "No, I don't think Kathleen would mind driving the pickup." Judy looked at her companion quizzically.

"Whatever it is, I'm game," Kathleen answered the unspoken question.

"Okay, Brad. We'll meet you there in about an hour." She paused again. "Yeah, I'll bring my goosenecks and the extra block and tackle."

Kathleen was completely mystified.

"Goodbye," Judy said just before hanging up the phone and returning to her breakfast.

"What are we going to do?" Kathleen asked.

"Pull a well," Judy answered.

They both continued eating. Kathleen had no idea what pulling a well meant, but she was growing to accept the necessity of learning as she went. It wasn't such a bad way of living.

⁂

"It's about time," Brad called as he rose from the pickup seat where he'd been taking a nap.

"We had important stuff to do," Judy answered as she leaned out the driver's window of her own pickup.

"Like what?"

"Like finish breakfast."

"That's okay then, just so it was important." He smiled the lopsided grin that was Brad's trademark.

Both women, and their dogs, got out of the pickup, and Judy walked straight to the windmill tower near where they had parked. She quickly took stock of the dangerously low water level. If they didn't get the well repaired today, she'd need to help Brad haul water at least two times a day from the well in her nearby north pasture.

"So she won't pump," Judy said.

"Not a drop. Pipe sounds like the well has a bad case of gas, but no water."

"Must be the leathers."

Brad turned to Kathleen. "Do you have any idea

what we're talking about?"

"Some. Judy told me about leathers the first few days I was here."

"Good. I was afraid when you heard Judy mention leathers that you'd think we were talking 'S and M' here."

"From Judy? No way. Now if it had been you, Brad…"

"Damn, and I thought you had a good opinion of me." Brad stood close to Kathleen and placed a hand on her shoulder. Kathleen moved away. Unconsciously, she stood closer to Judy.

The muscles in Judy's jaw tightened noticeably.

"Kathleen, this is going to be a whole lot easier with you helping," Judy said.

"Sure is," Brad said. "Pa would be here, but he and Ma went to Amarillo for the weekend."

"Sounds romantic," Judy said.

"Can parents be romantic?" Brad asked.

"Yours do a pretty good job of it," Judy said.

Brad grinned devilishly and looked directly at Kathleen. "I guess that goes to prove that I've had good training."

Judy took Kathleen's arm lightly and led her to a spot at the base of the windmill tower. Both women ignored Brad.

"Here's what we do," Judy said. "Brad and I will go up the tower to hook up the block and tackle. Then we unhook the sucker rods from the mill itself, and we use the block and tackle to pull the well one rod at a time."

"Can you do that by hand?" Kathleen asked.

"No. That's why we need you. You'll be driving the pickup, while Brad and I handle the sucker rods."

"Oh," Kathleen said, confused.

"Don't worry. I'll ride with you the first few sections. It will all become clear to you, as you see it done."

"Sure," Kathleen said, apprehensive.

Brad and Judy began the familiar task of setting up stands for the sucker rods, and Kathleen watched and learned, doing her best to help. When Brad and Judy began the precarious climb up the tower, Brad with the block and tackle tied around his waist with a strong cord, and Judy with a full tool belt, Kathleen found it difficult to watch. Once, Judy's foot slipped, and Kathleen had trouble breathing for a good two minutes afterward.

"Is that as dangerous as it looks?" Kathleen called.

"Yes," Brad answered in the vertical distance between them. The smile he flashed toward her did little to ease Kathleen's apprehension.

Judy said nothing. She didn't want to break her concentration. It had been years since she had been aware of the danger of this task. As she felt Kathleen's eyes watching, Judy was suddenly aware of the horror she would cause Kathleen should she accidently fall. The awareness made her especially careful.

Before long, the preparatory tasks were finished. Brad attached a cable to the frame of the pickup, and they were ready to go.

Judy was right. The job was easier to understand by doing than through explanation. Judy only rode with Kathleen the first four or five of the trips of ten yards back then ten yards forward. The pickup's power pulled up one section of sucker rod. Kathleen waited, while Brand and Judy disconnected that rod then eased forward as they laid that rod to the side. After they connected the next section to the cable, Kathleen backed the same ten yards once again.

Soon, all three worked in a steady routine. Kathleen drove, while Brad and Judy worked as a sweaty team, in perfect unison, as they plied gooseneck wrenches or moved rod. The same movements were repeated time after time, and Kathleen enjoyed the sight of two strong bodies, especially Judy's, in a symphony of motion. They were soon covered in sweat, grease, and dirt, but they continued to work. It was almost a surprise when the last length of rod was pulled from the hole, and the pumping mechanism was finally in their grasp. Kathleen watched in amazement as the actual job of changing the leathers took only a few moments. Then they began the tedious task of reversing the job. One by one, the rods went back into the hole, each one tightened by hand before the next section could be attached.

It was hours into the day, and there had been no break for lunch. Brad and Judy hoped to have the well running before the mid-day winds were completely gone. Kathleen, with the relatively easy job of driving, was beginning to feel the strain of the constant concentration required to move only when needed and only as far as needed. She watched with concern as Judy and Brad's movements took on the sluggishness of exhaustion. Wrenches began to slip, although they were both still painfully careful when a goosenecked wrench was all that kept the lengths of rod from falling to the bottom of the hole—any well man's nightmare. Both the man and the woman swore with added vigor when the task did not go easily. Once, Kathleen opened the door of the pickup and stepped outside with the intention of suggesting a break, but Brad motioned to her crossly, and Kathleen lowered yet another rod.

It seemed like the job took forever. In reality, the three workers used less than an hour to replace the rods to the well. Judy and Brad looked almost immediately to the job of reconnecting the rods to the mill, but Kathleen intervened. She retrieved the thermos of coffee from the pickup seat and a box of cheese-filled crackers from the stash Judy kept behind the seat.

The pair grumbled at the delay, but they also consumed the crackers and cheese with gusto, ignoring the filthy hands that held them. Once they'd each drunk a cup of coffee and had a short rest, leaning against the edge of the water tank, Kathleen no longer sensed the edge of exhaustion that she had detected in both of them. She was still anxious about them going back up the tower.

"Let's do it," Judy said, as she crumpled the cellophane packet and tossed it back into the now empty cracker box.

"Yeah," Brad agreed, without energy.

"Can I go up and help?" Kathleen asked. "Driving isn't that tough. I'm more rested than you two."

Judy smiled with limited energy. "Kathleen, you learn as fast as anybody I've ever seen, but this isn't a job that's learned overnight. You could help by picking up the rod stands and putting the wrenches back in the tool box. Whatever you do, don't stand under the tower while we're working. I'd hate to drop something on you."

Kathleen took the cracker box from Judy. As she stood in front of the woman, Kathleen raised a hand

and touched Judy's face.

"Be careful," Kathleen said.

"Jesus Christ!" Brad erupted in anger.

Both women looked at him in surprise.

"What's eating you?" Judy asked.

"Not a damn thing! Let's get this over with."

With an energy born of anger, Brad started up the tower, the cord he would use to carry down the block already tied to his waist. Judy grabbed the tool belt and started up after him.

Kathleen couldn't watch. She busied herself collecting stands and tools, getting the tools from near the wellhead, while Brad and Judy were still climbing the tower. She wanted to be well clear of the area while the longtime friends worked high above the ground. Kathleen did not want Judy to spare any concentration worrying about anything but her own safety.

It took longer for them to rehook the mill than it had to disconnect it. Neither Judy nor Brad were fools. They knew they were tired, and they worked with all the more caution because of it.

Kathleen did not breathe with complete ease until they were on the ground again. As soon as they reached earth, Brad threw down his hat and plunged his full face into the green-tinged water of the stock tank. The well was now pumping cool, clear water.

"Don't come up with any leeches, will you," Judy said.

Brad coughed and sputtered as he rose and shook water from his hair. "That felt good enough to be worth a leech."

The muscles in Judy's arms quivered as she placed the tool belt in the tool box in the back of her pickup. Useless and Somegood were already in the pickup bed. They'd given up chasing rabbits hours before, and they both whined with the desire to go home.

"You still mad?" Judy asked of the dripping Brad.

"Naw," he answered.

"What was eating at you?"

"Nothing, just tired I guess."

Judy looked at him closely. She hadn't often seen the good-natured Brad erupt in anger.

"Okay, whatever you say. Since your folks are gone, do you want to come over for dinner?" Judy smiled at the other woman. "Kathleen's cooking."

"Thanks, no. I just want to go home. Ma left lots of leftovers in the freezer."

Judy opened her pickup door and started to step inside. Kathleen was already in her seat.

"Maybe another day," Judy said.

"Yeah, maybe," Brad answered. "Oh, ladies."

"Ladies?" Judy asked. She was expecting Brad to come back with one of his habitual one-liners.

"Yeah, I said ladies. Thanks for all your help."

"Anytime," Judy responded.

"I enjoyed it," Kathleen said.

Without another word, Brad climbed into his pickup and drove away.

"I wonder what's bothering him," Judy said.

Chapter Twelve

I take it I'm cooking," Kathleen said as she used the wooden bootjack to free her tired feet.

"That's what I told Brad. You wouldn't want to make a liar out of me, would you?" Judy answered as she used the battle-worn bar of Lava soap to scrub away a layer of the day's grime.

"God forbid. We have any meat thawed?"

"Hamburger."

"How about spaghetti?"

Judy eye's closed in ecstasy at the thought.

"Sounds wonderful." She glanced at Kathleen, concerned. "You aren't one of those folks who thinks you have to cook with fresh tomatoes and let it simmer half the day?"

Kathleen smiled. "Sometimes, but not today. It should be ready in an hour or so."

Judy whooped in joy.

A spontaneous laugh gave Kathleen's face a soft set of wrinkles around her eyes and mouth. Judy liked the look.

"Why don't you take a shower while I cook?" Kathleen suggested.

Judy lifted her arm and took a quick sniff. "That bad, huh?"

"Yep."

"Okay, but I'll make it quick," Judy said as she left the kitchen.

Kathleen was at home in the farmhouse kitchen, and she did like to cook. By the time Judy returned, freshly scrubbed and dressed in a t-shirt and gym shorts, the sauce was bubbling in one pan and pasta boiling in another.

"Smells wonderful," Judy announced. "Is it ready?"

"As soon as we get the table set."

Kathleen drained the water from the pasta as Judy placed silverware and plates on the table. After she finished draining the spaghetti, Kathleen watched Judy with open admiration. Years of work and survival in the harsh beauty of ranch life had given Judy a well-muscled body and an animal grace. Her arms were brown, but her legs were pale and creamy, marked only by the leftover indentions from her boot tops. Judy's short, brown hair was still wet from the shower and hung like a ruff around her face. Kathleen noticed, with interest, that Judy had not bothered to don a bra after leaving the shower. She liked the shape she saw beneath the t-shirt.

As Judy placed the last knife, she looked up to meet Kathleen's open gaze. An embarrassed flush appeared beneath her scattering of freckles.

"Like what you see?" Judy asked.

"Yes."

Judy laughed, trying to hide her embarrassment. Kathleen emptied the pasta into a waiting bowl and picked up a plate to fill it with pasta and sauce. Both women claimed sizeable servings and ate in silence. Judy paused once, in the process of emptying her plate, to leave the table and start a pot of coffee.

"I feel human again," Judy said, as she laid her fork in her empty plate and leaned back comfortably.

"I should ask you to cook more often. You're good."

"What do you mean ask?" Kathleen grinned mischievously. "It was more like a royal decree."

Judy grinned in return. "Hey, a woman's home is her castle."

"We were out in the pasture," Kathleen responded.

"Don't be picky. I'm trying to compliment your food."

"Thanks."

Judy's eyes narrowed as she thought. "I now know you're a good cook and a good sport. When are you going to let me see how good you are at writing?"

"When are you going to let me see more of your art?"

Judy looked in the general direction of the living room. "Most of the good stuff is already framed and hanging, or was long ago sold or given away. I'll let you see the professional portfolio I used in Dallas, anytime you want."

"Do you still draw or paint?"

A crease crossed Judy's forehead. "Sometimes. When I knew you were coming to stay, I was inspired to do a watercolor. Don't know why I haven't shown it to you yet. I was shy at first, and then I forgot. Seems like, since I came back to the farm, I just haven't had the need...or maybe it's the heart. When the time comes, I'll paint again."

"You've got talent. You need to keep it up."

"Hey, you haven't answered my question. When are you going to let me read some of your writing?"

"You've read some of my articles."

Judy leaned close and rested her hand on Kathleen's. "Is that where your heart is?" Judy asked.

Kathleen looked deep into the blue of Judy's

eyes.

"No," she answered.

"I know you're working on something on that portable computer of yours. Surely it's not just the *Cosmo* article."

Kathleen played with her fork. "Yeah, the articles pay the bills, but I guess I'm predictable as a writer. We all have poetry, a novel, or a play deep in our hearts, waiting to be let free."

"What about those writers who have set the novel free?"

"Another one is always in hiding. Once you finish one, there's a little voice whispering of yet another."

"How many novels have you written?"

Kathleen looked surprised. "How did you know I'd written any? I haven't had any published." For a second, a hint of suspicion crossed Kathleen's face. "No, you're not the type to go through my things when I'm not here."

Both women placed their plates in the sink and filled cups with coffee that they then took to the living room.

Judy paused in thought before she answered Kathleen's question.

"Don't rightly know how I knew you wrote novels. I've suspected it since the first day I met you. You seem like you ought to be writing a novel, that's all." Judy sat comfortably on the sofa and brazenly placed her bare feet on the coffee table. "It's in the way you think, and you're constantly watching people, not just for their ideas, but for little things, the things that make them people, not just subjects."

"Okay, I'll buy that."

"So, when you going to do it?"

"Do what?"

"Let me see some of your writing," Judy said, exasperated.

"You've read some of my articles."

"Shit, here we are back at square one." Judy sighed. "I mean some of your real writing."

Kathleen stirred coffee that was already stirred. "You want to see my novel?"

"Any one of them, yes, I do," Judy answered.

"I've only got the one I'm working on with me, and it isn't finished."

"That's okay. I'd still like to see what you've written."

"Why? You won't know how the story ends."

Judy set her cup on the table and leaned to rest her arm on the back of the sofa. She brushed a wayward tuft of hair from Kathleen's face.

"I want to see what I can of you in what you write."

Kathleen's breathing became shallow. "That's what I'm afraid of."

Judy cupped Kathleen's chin in her hand and turned Kathleen's face until she could look directly into the other woman's eyes.

"If I were an editor, would you be afraid?" Judy asked.

"I'm not falling in love with an editor," Kathleen whispered.

Anything but a kiss would have been inappropriate. Judy behaved appropriately. The kiss was long and gentle, but Judy did not forget her purpose. She pulled away so that she could see Kathleen more clearly.

"Go get your book," Judy commanded.

"My portable printer is pretty bad. I only make a hard copy as an emergency backup. It's difficult to read."

"Kathleen! Trust me. Get your book."

Kathleen did as she was told. In the end, it wasn't that difficult. After all, it was really what she wanted to do. She handed Judy the manuscript, well-marked and dog-eared, at least in the early chapters. Judy opened the paper cover and read the title, *In Memory of Others*.

"Sounds interesting," Judy said and then began to read in earnest.

Kathleen sat beside her like a kitten in the dog pen. She fiddled and twitched, carried empty cups to the kitchen, and then returned to fiddle and twitch again.

Dragging her gaze from the page, Judy looked at Kathleen.

"You're making me nervous," Judy said. "You've had a hot, sweaty day, too. Why don't you go take a shower?"

"Good idea. I've never felt comfortable watching someone read my stuff."

"No lie. I never would have guessed," Judy said with gentle sarcasm.

"Okay, I can take a hint."

Kathleen left, and Judy read.

The concept behind the book immediately captured Judy's interest. A retired sociology professor, moves to a small Colorado town because of its beauty, obscurity, and quaintness. Out of curiosity, she attends a town meeting. She enjoys watching the interaction between the townspeople, and the family feel of the group. The town faces a crucial period because of changes in the mining around which the town had been built a century earlier and the approaches of a recreational developer. Quietly, she offers her expertise on a minor, related subject.

Before she knows what's happened, those attending the town meeting unanimously elect her mayor. With the town's people leaving in a departure more like a retreat, the former mayor happily passes on the symbols of office, including a uniquely structured ring.

It's a magic ring, a ring that enables the spirits of those long dead to advise the community's leader. The woman's desire for a quiet life suddenly turns into a unique existence that she finds both terrifying and compelling.

At first, Judy saw Kathleen on every page, in every word, but that soon passed. The story and the characters took on life, and she was soon lost in the tale, an observer in a new reality. When Kathleen returned from the shower, Judy barely noticed. Kathleen brought fresh coffee for them both and retrieved a paperback novel from her room. As Judy continued to read, Kathleen read her own book. Her anxiety passed. It was replaced by a feeling of warmth at the thought of sharing with Judy something so basic to her very self.

The hours passed and the pages turned. Judy got up once to go to the bathroom, but neither woman said a word. They were both reluctant to shatter the atmosphere hanging heavy in the room. Other than that one break, Judy read without stopping, not because she felt obligated to do so, but because she was enjoying the book. The evening passed, and the night grew dark. Kathleen became engrossed in the John Irving novel she was reading so that time passed quickly for both of them.

Finally, Judy turned the last page and stared at the back cover in hopes of reading something that wasn't there. The crickets were singing their nightly song and the late news would have been heard, if either woman had wanted to turn on the television.

"What do you think?" Kathleen asked breathlessly.

"You were right. I'm frustrated."

"You didn't like it?" Kathleen was anxious.

"God, no! I loved it. I'm frustrated because I want to know what happens."

Kathleen laughed. "I've got an outline you can read, but it won't do you much good. The outline is just a skeleton, and my books rarely turn out exactly the way I plan."

"I'd rather wait. I want to read your story with all its flesh and depth."

"You really like it?"

They were both sitting on the couch, their knees barely touching in an unspoken need for contact. Judy moved close and placed her arm around Kathleen's shoulders.

"I like it most because of what I see of you. You write beautifully, Kathleen, and I don't think anybody can do that unless there's a beautiful person behind the words."

The affection they had both delayed expressing throughout the evening now came to the forefront. They kissed and touched and moved to positions greatly increasing the comfort and pleasure of both. Kathleen couldn't have said how she knew when it was, but they reached that point of passion and intimacy where Judy had pulled away before, and Kathleen silently prepared herself for it to happen again. It didn't. Instead, Judy's hands explored Kathleen's body with greater daring, while her tongue tasted her mouth. Kathleen moaned in pleasure as Judy's hand found its way to her breast, and Judy's fingers formed a gentle cup around the soft fullness. Judy nuzzled against Kathleen's neck.

"Do you remember what I said last night?" Judy whispered.

"Every word," Kathleen answered.

"Guess what."

"What?"

"It wasn't just my body doing the talking."

Judy gently pushed away and stood shakily. She took Kathleen by the hand and pulled the other woman to her feet. Judy held that hand tightly as she led the way to her bedroom.

They climbed between the coolness of the clean sheets. It would be well into the early hours of the morning before either of them slept. They eventually dozed, exhausted and replete with pleasure.

It would be the last night Kathleen spent in Judy's bed.

Not that they wouldn't continue to share each other's beings and please each other's bodies. This was only the first of many nights together, but it would never again be in Judy's bed for some time during that first night, a miracle happened. Sometime, as they lay together, a magic wand waved a transformation.

In the morning, they awoke and Judy's bed was gone. In its place stood their bed—a five foot by six foot haven where they shared passion, pleasure, and especially intimacy. It was a place where they would speak in quiet voices, reluctant to let their voices travel beyond the tiny world that was theirs and theirs alone.

In this healing place, old tears fell from the well where they were stagnated and forgotten. Old wounds bled only to feel the healing touch of a lover's heart.

Sometimes the gentle whispers were punctuated by the staccato sound of laughter or calls of passion, when the joy they felt could not be contained in the five by six bubble of their bed. At those moments, a burst of light erupted from a core of gold, and with that nova of happiness the birds sang with greater joy, while Useless and Somegood smiled their doggie smiles and dreamed their doggie dreams.

Kathleen's *Cosmo* article was finished, submitted, and accepted. Still, she stayed. Judy didn't ask. She simply accepted whatever happiness she was given.

Chapter Thirteen

Judy threw the come-along and fencing pliers into the toolbox and slammed the lid closed. Kathleen carried the coffee can full of fencing staples into the pickup cab, so that it would be handy the next time it was needed. Fence building and repair was an ongoing activity on any ranch. The coffee can normally lived in a little niche on the floorboard of the cluttered cab of Judy's pickup.

As she entered the pickup cab, Kathleen carefully searched the horizon, looking for any approaching vehicles. None were to be seen, and Kathleen quickly pulled herself across the pickup seat to a spot just beside Judy. When Judy leaned forward to start the engine, Kathleen wrapped her arms around her lover. Judy laughed as she placed the gear stick in neutral and leaned back to accept Kathleen's kiss.

The kiss was slow and sensual, as their tongues played against lips and teeth, and the two women enjoyed the now familiar taste of each other. When the kiss ended, Kathleen relaxed to a comfortable position with her face nestled between Judy's breasts. Judy, also relaxed, leaned her head against the back of the seat and used one hand to stroke the soft French braid of Kathleen's dark brown hair. The chug of the pickup's engine wasn't the only motor running. Moving only one hand, Kathleen undid the top button of Judy's shirt. She pushed the material to one side and nibbled at the top edge of Judy's breast.

"Mmm, salty," Kathleen said.

"Of course I'm salty. I've been sweating. I probably smell ripe, too."

Kathleen buried her face in Judy's chest and moved until her nose was resting under Judy's arm.

"I love the way you smell," Kathleen said.

"No accounting for taste," Judy said as she laughed. She gently pulled Kathleen upright so they could kiss again. "Let's go home and take a shower," Judy said.

"And then make love."

Another kiss was Kathleen's answer.

"Lordie! How do we still manage to get so much work done when we spend so much time in bed?" Judy asked.

"Maybe its leftover sexual energy," Kathleen said as she moved ever so slightly away from her lover.

"Maybe so."

Judy placed the pickup in gear, and they rattled across the pasture toward the house. As they drove out of the pasture and onto the county road, Kathleen moved even farther from her lover. They still maintained contact. Kathleen's hand rested on the back of Judy's neck, while Judy, when she wasn't shifting gears, caressed Kathleen's knee and thigh. But no one, seeing them from a distance, would wonder at the two women sitting side by side. If another pickup approached, they need only move slightly to obtain a more circumspect appearance. It was a practice they had developed early in their relationship as lovers. Over the weeks, it had become a habit.

For several miles they rode in comfortable silence. Neither woman felt the need for idle conversation.

They were at ease with each other.

"Can we stop and see Miss Sally and Baby before we go to the house?" Kathleen asked.

"Whatever you want, honey," Judy answered.

Sally Doc Bar and her filly were living in the pasture behind the house. Judy and Kathleen had made a regular ritual of filling one of the ranch's ubiquitous coffee cans with oats, to feed to Miss Sally. The women took turns feeding the mare while the other woman fondled, played with, and generally enjoyed the rapidly growing filly. Baby was playful and affectionate, and the frequent handling was rapidly overcoming the young horse's natural fear of humans. The wild-eyed filly had even accepted Useless and Somegood as members of her herd. As the women returned to the ranch headquarters, they looked forward to the simple joy of time with the filly.

The pickup rattled into the yard, and Judy parked in her usual place inside the barn. They both got out and Judy hit the button to lower the overhead door as they stepped outside.

"Let's go see Baby," Kathleen said.

"You go ahead. I'll get the oats and meet you there."

Judy opened the door to the feed shed and was just filling a coffee can with grain, when she heard Kathleen call her name. There was something in her lover's voice that made Judy's heart rate increase. She quickly left the shed and crossed the yard at a trot. Once she rounded the corner of the barn, she could see the cause of Kathleen's concern.

Miss Sally and the filly were approximately one hundred yards from the house. The mare stood protectively over the filly. Baby was obviously struggling to stand. Now that they were listening, the women could hear the mare's nickers of encouragement and the colt's cries of pain.

"What's wrong with Baby?" Kathleen asked, a note of panic in her voice.

"I don't know," Judy answered. There was a ring of fear to her words as well. "Let's go see."

Kathleen climbed through the fence.

"Wait." Judy placed her hand on Kathleen's arm. "We better take the pickup."

The women ran back to the barn, and Judy fumbled anxiously with her keys as she opened the side door. Kathleen caught the button to open the overhead door, as she ran around the back of the pickup to the passenger side. Judy had the pickup started and was backing out the opening before the door had fully risen. The radio antenna flopped and thwanged as it made contact with the bottom of the rising door.

Kathleen was out of the pickup and opening the gate, before Judy rolled to a halt. Kathleen dropped the gate and jumped back into the pickup as Judy paused, as she drove over the wire gate

The mare trotted in a nervous circle around her foal and neighed, obviously calling for assistance, to the approaching pickup. As they drew near, the situation became painfully obvious. The filly lay near a prairie dog hole with the dirt around the hole freshly churned. Both women were heartsick at the sight of the young horse's twisted right foreleg. The filly was determined to stand, but every time she attempted to place weight on the leg, she fell and screamed in pain.

"God, I can't listen," Kathleen said as she placed her hands over her ears.

"Jesus, help us," was Judy's only response.

They stopped the pickup, and Judy ran to the filly's side. She knelt on the horse's shoulder, making it impossible for the filly to rise. For an instant, the mare bared her teeth at the woman who was her mistress and friend. Seeing the mare's distress, the two dogs kept their distance. Eventually, they left the scene for a safe haven in the hay shed. Kathleen took her hands from her ears, and walked to Sally Doc Bar.

"It's all right, Miss Sally. We just want to help." Kathleen's voice quavered, matching the tears that were already trickling down her cheeks.

Judy stroked the filly's neck and spoke soft, senseless phrases to calm the panicked animal. With an experienced hand, Judy felt down the shoulder and then the leg, pausing to touch with greater detail an area half way between hock and knee.

"Jesus, God Almighty," Judy said.

"How bad is it?" Kathleen asked.

"Bad enough," Judy answered. Her jaw was locked in an expression of determination. "I need you to come hold Baby down."

Kathleen left the mare and took Judy's position kneeling on the filly's shoulder. Judy walked back to the pickup and fished out the halter she kept in the toolbox. She walked gently to the nervous mare and deftly placed the lead rope around Miss Sally's neck. Once the horse was semisecured, Judy fastened the halter around the mare's head and then led her to the pickup, where she tied the lead rope to the bumper.

"I need you to lead Miss Sally back to the barn." There was an edge to Judy's voice, a hardness that Kathleen had never heard before.

"Why?" Kathleen's anxiety was increasing.

"I don't want either you or the mare seeing this."

Judy moved to the pickup cab and rummaged behind the seat. She retrieved the catch rope she kept there. Judy laid the rope on the seat and then pulled the .30-30 Winchester from its protective cover.

"What do you think you're doing?" Kathleen demanded.

Judy turned, fire and determination flashing in her eyes.

"What has to be done," she answered.

"You're not going to shoot Baby," Kathleen said. It was a statement, not a question.

"Kathleen, listen to me. The bone is completely broken in two pieces. If it was a fracture, we might could do something, but it's not. It's a bad break."

In a protective gesture, Kathleen moved to lie on top of the filly. The young horse quieted even more, taking comfort in the physical contact.

"Goddamn you, Judy Proctor! You're not going to kill this animal just because you don't want to pay a vet bill," Kathleen yelled. The injured filly was startled by the anger in the woman's voice and began to struggle until Kathleen gently petted her neck.

Judy's face reddened. "You think I want to do this?" she said, waving the rifle in front of her.

"It's the modern age. It can't be that you just shoot horses for a broken leg," Kathleen said. "I've read about race horses..."

"That's different," Judy answered.

"Why?" Kathleen had the killer look of a mother protecting her young. "Because they're worth more money."

"Jesus, Kathleen. If the horse was worth a million

dollars, they'd have to kill it with a break this bad."

"Doctors can do so much now. Why can't the leg be set and put in a cast?"

"Kathleen, horses aren't like people. They have to stand up. If they can't stand up, they die. It's a long, slow death, but they do die."

"I can't believe that. Maybe we could make a sling."

"Kathleen…"

"Would you shoot me because I broke a leg?" Kathleen's anger turned vicious. "Or would you just dump me for a healthy woman?"

Judy looked as though she had taken a punch full in the stomach. Her face went so pale that, for an instant, Kathleen was afraid her lover would be sick.

"Kathleen, how can you…" Judy paced absently beside the pickup. Finally, she shoved the rifle back in its sheath and slammed the pickup door.

"I'll lead the mare back to the corrals and call the vet," Judy said. "Can you stay with the filly?"

Kathleen was crying as much in relief as fear. "Yes, of course."

Judy untied the lead rope and began a rapid walk toward the still open gate. Kathleen watched anxiously as the mare briefly fought her mistress, shaking her head and balking at the prospect of leaving her injured foal. For a moment, Kathleen feared that the mare would rear and strike at Judy with her forefeet. Judy saw the danger before it became reality, and a timely jerk on the lead rope halted the near revolt.

"Easy, Miss Sally," Judy said as she caressed the mare's velvety nose. "We'll take care of her." It still took another jerk or two on the lead, but the mare finally followed. As she watched her lover depart,

Kathleen leaned against the injured filly, both giving and receiving comfort from the animal.

The wait seemed to take forever. The vet needed time to gather the medicines and supplies he might need and to make the forty minute drive from town. Judy returned as soon as she finished the phone call, and both women occupied themselves comforting the anxious filly. Kathleen stayed at the horse's shoulder, while Judy sat on the ground, the filly's head resting in her lap. There was a charged silence between the women. Kathleen could feel Judy's coldness like a solid wall. Somewhere in the back of her heart and mind, Kathleen knew and regretted the pain she had caused her lover. But for the moment, all of her energy was directed to Baby.

It was more than an hour before they saw the vet's pickup leave the highway and make its dusty way down the county road. The vet knew the way. He drove directly to the horse pasture and toward the women and the injured filly.

The special pickup, organized into a portable clinic with different sections for various medications and equipment, pulled to a halt just a few feet away. Doc Burnes, climbed out of the cab, his bald and sunburned head glistening in the sunlight.

"Looks like you've had some bad luck, Judy," the kindly vet said.

"Not one of my better days. That's for sure. Doc, do you remember Kathleen Romero?" Judy didn't bother to look at her lover when she spoke her name.

"Sure do. She helped us when we Bang's tested your cows." He opened a compartment in the back of his pickup and pulled out a black case. "How bad is it broke?"

"Pretty bad, Doc," Judy said.

The vet walked slowly toward the filly, careful not to startle the animal. Years of practice taught him not to begin the examination of a prone horse from the business end of the hooves. Kathleen moved to the side as he took her place at the shoulder.

"Don't look so good," he said.

Just as Judy had done, he gently ran his hand down the filly's leg, pausing to feel more closely, a spot between the hoof and knee.

"Judy, why did you call me? I think you already know what needs to be done."

Kathleen gave a strangled cry, and her hands flew to her face.

"Oh well, I guess an injection is an easier way to go anyway," the vet said. "I'll get what I need from the pickup."

Kathleen left for the house at a dead run. Judy could hear Kathleen's sobs, but she let her lover go. Instead, she took the vet's place at the filly's shoulder and used her weight to keep the injured animal on the ground.

The drug worked quickly. It wasn't long before Kathleen heard the vet's pickup pull out of the yard and back onto the county road. She was still lying full-length across their bed, sobs racking her body, when she heard Judy's pickup as it stopped inside the barn. A few minutes later, Kathleen heard the rumble and sputter of the John Deere tractor. Her sobs eased. Slowly, other thoughts and feelings replaced the maternal instinct that had filled her the moment she saw the injured filly.

A reddish glow was forming on the horizon when Kathleen left the house, walked through the yard, climbed through the fence, and made her way toward the sound of the tractor. Judy was using the front-end loader to dig a grave near where the filly lay dead. When Judy saw her lover approaching, she killed the motor on the tractor and sat watching, apparently mesmerized by Kathleen's approach. Kathleen stood beside the tractor, desperately needing Judy to cross the remaining distance between them.

Judy's face was tightly closed, and her eyes flashed fire and ice as she pushed open the door to the cab and lowered herself to the ground. They stood facing each other, not touching, a coldness still between them.

"Are you okay?" Judy asked.

"No. Are you?"

"No." Judy's face tensed even more. "How could you think... Did you really mean..."

There were tears coursing down Kathleen's face.

"Judy, I would have said anything to stop you from shooting Baby."

"I didn't want to. You know that, don't you?"

"Yes, I know. I knew then."

"It had to be done."

"I know. I just..."

"God, Kathleen. You hurt me like no one's hurt me before. Not even when Sandy and I split did I..."

"Do you remember what you told me about Sandy? About when you first moved back here?"

"She just wouldn't believe that I had to come home. That I still loved her, but I had to be here."

"I think I now understand what she felt...why she reacted that way."

"Why?" Judy asked.

"When I saw the filly...I just couldn't...Judy,

you're naturally strong. You don't understand. Sometimes, people refuse to see the truth just because it's painful."

Judy shook with emotion. Kathleen was frightened by the lack of color in her lover's face.

"When you said that you thought I'd leave you because you were hurt I…"

"I know better than that, Judy. They were just words…anything to save the filly." Kathleen glanced at the cold form of the foal. "Instead, I prolonged her pain."

"I love you, Kathleen."

"And I love you."

Judy's sobs started, and, suddenly, the cold thing between them was gone. The lovers held each other closely, and they cried together as the daylight faded around them. The purple light caressed them, offering the simple comfort of a summer evening. They enjoyed that little gift from God. Besides, they had each other. Both pain and pleasure were all the better for that.

Chapter Fourteen

It's about time you showed up around here," Deb Monroe said, as she snapped the cap on the pen she had been using.

"Sorry, Deb, old girl. We've been kind of busy," Judy answered. She took a seat in one of the two sixty-year-old chairs resting in front of Deb's desk, while Kathleen hesitantly sat in the other.

Deb's eyes darted back and forth between her two visitors. The intense curiosity that served her so well in the newspaper business was obviously turned toward the two women.

"Judy Proctor, you do know that when we decided to have weekly lunches, that meant we were supposed to go out once a week, not once a month?"

Judy blushed. "Don't tell you me you've been starving to death waiting for me to buy you enchiladas."

Deb looked down at her stout form, a shape that had spread slightly in recent years. "Sure I have. Can't you tell by looking?"

"You're just wasting away."

"That's why I like you so much, Judy Proctor. Your powers of observation." Deb turned to Kathleen. "You still liking life in the country?"

"Very much," Kathleen answered. "I never thought it could be so gratifying to build fence."

"Lord, Judy. Have you taken that woman's temperature? I think she's ill."

"If she is, I've got the same condition," Judy answered.

Deb's eyes flashed as she looked hard at Judy's face. "I'll just bet you do." There was a flicker of amusement in her expression. As Judy's blush deepened, Deb dropped her pen on the desk and took her purse out of the bottom drawer.

"Let's go eat before I really do start wasting away." Deb began straightening the orderly mess on her desk. "Kathleen, when I sent you out to the Proctor place, you weren't supposed to steal my best friend."

Kathleen tried not to blush. Her efforts just increased the color. "Sorry, Deb. It's just that she's such good company."

Deb stood and walked around the desk toward the door. "Don't let me give you a hard time. Truth is, I'm glad Judy's got somebody out there with her. I'd go batshit from the loneliness if I were her."

"How'd Hank take it when you said you wouldn't be home for dinner?" Judy asked. Her attempt to change the subject worked with ease.

"He wanted to know if chili dogs were okay for the kids."

"Is he picking up Laura and Carl from the sitter?"

"Yep. All things considered, he's a pretty decent husband. Now, if I could just get him to change deodorants."

"You're lucky," Kathleen said as she held the office door for the other women. "A lot of men wouldn't dream of spending an evening caring for their children while their wife went out with the girls."

"He helped make 'em. He can help look after 'em. That's how I feel about it." Deb took her key ring out of her purse and, as the last one to leave the office, carefully locked the door. "Besides, he assumed I was covering a special city council or county commission meeting. I didn't bother to tell him otherwise."

Judy laughed. "That's my Deb."

When they reached Kathleen's Escort, Judy opened the passenger door and crawled into the back seat, leaving the front for the longer-legged Deb.

"Do you remember how to get to J & S?" Judy asked, as Kathleen started the car.

Kathleen smiled as she pulled away from the curb. "This isn't exactly Denver," she answered.

"Well, shoot, Kathleen. If you don't know the way, you might be lost for all of ten, fifteen minutes. We wouldn't want to cause you any anxiety," Deb said.

Kathleen laughed. "I'll live."

They rode in companionable silence for the few minutes it took Kathleen to make the simple trek to the home of the World's Greatest Enchiladas. Of course, Judy and Kathleen had already shared their joint secret about the superiority of the chicken variety to be had in El Paso, but they weren't going to risk being tarred and feathered by sharing that information with the rest of the town.

On a Wednesday evening, the restaurant was relatively quiet. Mid-week prayer meeting was a tradition for most of the town, and drew many families. Other families were just at home, trying not to call attention to the fact that they were not attending mid-week church service. Both Deb and Judy were among the small group tolerated by the community as the necessary number of dedicated pagans. Among other things, that meant they had J & S to themselves on Wednesday nights. Paganism did have its appeal.

Conversation was animated throughout the

meal. Deb brought the country visitors up-to-date on the gossip behind the stories they read in her weekly paper, and Judy and Kathleen told an abbreviated tale of the death of Baby. Through it all, Deb's unasked question hung in the air like a layer of smoke.

"You and Brad been working together much lately?" Deb asked Judy.

Judy paused as she made a detailed search of her recent memory. "Come to think of it, I haven't seen much of him since that day we helped pull a well. That had to be two weeks ago."

"That's not like normal. You two have been thick as thieves since you were old enough to terrorize the countryside on your ponies."

"Lord, Deb. I'm glad you mentioned it. I guess I have been neglecting good, old Bradley."

Deb started to her mouth with a forkful of enchilada and then returned it to her plate. "When you do see him, I'd advise you to keep your head low."

"Why?"

"I ran into him last week."

"So?"

"I don't know what you did, but he's not real happy with you."

"What do you mean?" It was Kathleen who asked, an anxious note in her voice.

"I asked him how you were doing and if Kathleen was still out at the place. He told me he didn't waste his time keeping up with a pair of stuck-up women."

Judy temporarily forgot her meal. "I'd best give him a call. He seemed a little funny the day we pulled the well. Wonder what's eating him."

"Yeah, I wonder," Deb responded.

They sat for a long time over coffee after the meal.

In the end, they made a hasty departure after Judy glanced at her watch and reminded her companions that the movie started in fifteen minutes.

"What's showing?" Kathleen asked.

"I don't know," Judy answered.

Kathleen stopped mid stride in the parking lot. "We're going to a movie, and you don't even know what it is?"

Judy and Deb laughed.

"This isn't life in the city," Deb said.

"There's only one movie house," Judy added, "and we're only in town this one night."

"In the city, the decision is which movie to go see. In a small town, the decision is whether or not to go see the movie," Deb said.

Kathleen shook her head, amused. "I never thought about it."

"Don't worry, Kathleen. One of the perks of working for the newspaper is being able to see the movie ads early. I know what's on, and it's a decent flick."

When they arrived at the theater, Deb steered them pointedly to seats in the back, far from anyone else in the audience.

"We might want to talk about the actors," Deb explained.

As soon as they'd found their seats, Kathleen excused herself to find the restroom. Judy started to rise to show her lover the way, but Deb subtly grabbed her friend's shirt and pulled her back into her seat. With a sigh, Judy realized that it was time for the unasked question. Kathleen had barely stepped out of the auditorium when it came.

"You in love with her?" Deb asked.

"Yes."

"She in love with you?"

"Yes."

With the painful tenacity of the journalist, Deb bypassed the side issues and cut to the heart.

"She going to stay?"

The pain that crossed Judy's face made Deb wish she had eaten the last question.

"I don't know," Judy answered. She looked to the exit where she had last seen her lover with an expression of longing so intense that it was more of a prayer than a thought.

"Enjoy what you got," Deb said as she laid her hand on her best friend's arm. "If it's meant to be, it'll be."

Chapter Fifteen

Bird song traveled through the open windows like a gentle tickle from God, reminding the sleepers that a new day had come. Judy and Kathleen slept soundly, their bodies, unashamedly bare, wrapped comfortably around each other. Only a thin sheet protected them from the morning air. Their sleep was the sleep of the contented, undisturbed by troubled thoughts or violent emotions. They were at peace.

The dogs didn't bark, but then, why should they? The two women heard nothing as the pickup pulled into the yard. Their sleep continued as the visitor took the key from where it was hidden, over the rafters on the porch. It was not surprising he should know about the key. All the neighbors did, just as Judy knew where all her neighbors hid their keys. It was insurance during the violent winter storms that could send a stranded cowhand begging for shelter.

As the visitor opened the back door, both dogs, their tails happily wagging, rushed through for an early morning visit. It was the cold dampness of Useless's nose that awoke Kathleen.

At first, Kathleen thought it was a dream, an unwanted nightmare intruding on her peaceful slumber. Then, the haze of sleep faded from her vision, and she looked into the angry glare of the visitor's eyes.

"Judy, wake up," Kathleen said as she sat, the sheet held firmly to her chest.

In an instant, Judy had the nightstand drawer open and her hand on the pistol she kept there. Only then did she take time to look at the intruder.

"Bradley Kenton, what the hell are you doing here?" Judy yelled.

"I had to know. I just had to know," Brad said.

The tension in the air was thick. Useless barked once and Somegood whined. Both dogs were confused and undecided.

"Why didn't you just fucking ask?" Judy said, angry.

Brad's fist pounded the bedroom door as he turned and left the house at a run. Judy hastily pulled on the clothes she had left on a chair the night before. Kathleen jumped from bed and rummaged hastily for her own clothes.

"No," Judy said. "Stay here."

"But what if he…?"

"He won't. I need to go alone. He won't talk to me if I don't."

Judy was pulling her second boot onto a sockless foot as they heard Brad's pickup roar out of the yard and onto the road.

"Be careful," Kathleen said.

"I will," Judy called as she, too, ran from the house, grabbing her pickup keys from the peg in the kitchen, and her hat from the rack on the service porch.

It didn't take much of a tracker to find him. Despite his head start and excessive speed, his hasty progress raised a stream of dust that took its time about settling. Judy knew exactly where he had turned off the road and pulled into a pasture on the Kenton ranch. Despite his haste and anger, Brad had taken time to close the wire gate. Since there were no cattle in the pasture, Judy guessed that he was attempting to hide his tracks.

As she stepped out of the pickup and dropped the gate, Judy speculated on where he might be. Brad and his father were in the process of rebuilding a half mile of fence in the northwest corner of the pasture. She guessed that was where he had taken haven. Digging postholes had always been one of Brad's favorite ways to work off anger. Judy left the gate open. Unlike Brad, she wasn't trying to hide her tracks.

Judy was right. As she topped the rise, she spotted Brad's pickup. Even in the distance, she could see the rhythmic movement of the posthole digger. The Kenton's tractor was parked nearby, a power posthole tool attached, but Brad ignored it. His anger needed the pound and pull of the handheld diggers.

Brad didn't look up from his work as Judy got out of her pickup. Judy stood, uncomfortable in the angry silence.

"What was that stunt all about?" Judy finally asked.

Brad pulled the diggers from the hole with so much force that he knocked half the dirt back into the hole. When Judy realized his intentions, she dashed for the passenger door on his pickup. After he slammed the diggers into the back and jumped inside, Judy barely had time to get the door closed before the tires on the pickup began to spin, throwing dirt in a wide arc.

"Don't remember inviting you on this trip," Brad said.

"Since when do I need an invitation to go with you?"

"Please yourself."

Brad's lips were colorless from the tension, and his hands grasped the wheel with such force that the color of the skin alternated between red and white. The pickup bounced and rattled across the pasture as Brad expressed his anger with excessive speed. Judy expected him to turn toward the house, but, instead, he took a road, actually no more than a two-rut path, down into a canyon that marked the beginning of a government pasture. He didn't even slow as they rattled over a cattle guard.

"Slow down before you kill us both," Judy said.

"Doesn't sound like such a bad idea," Brad hissed.

The apprehension Judy felt turned into a cold, clear fear. She was relieved, as Brad slowed after hitting a particularly rigorous bump. The entire contents of the pickup bed rose in the air and, when the objects fell again, they were reshuffled like the pieces of a puzzle in a box.

"Brad, stop this damn pickup so we can talk."

He jammed the breaks, and the pickup stopped with as much anger and force as it had been driven.

"And what is it we've got to talk about?" Brad said. He leaned toward Judy. His eyes were red with emotion, and Judy swore she could smell the anger on him.

"Can you really tell me you hadn't guessed about me?"

"How was I to guess something like…like that?" Brad said.

"Good grief, Brad. Didn't you wonder why I

lived with Sandy so long?"

"I just figured you were…friends."

"We were, Brad."

Brad leaned close in a threat, not affection. "Than what are we?"

Judy looked at her hands and prayed to find the right words.

"Brad, my earliest memories of friendship are with you, but I've never…Jesus, Brad! What do you want us to be?"

He pounded at the steering wheel with the palms of his hand.

"Damn it, Judy! I want you to be my wife."

Judy felt the color drain from her face.

"Brad, I…"

"I've always wanted you to be the one to share my life, girl. Didn't you know?"

"Brad, buddy, you're my best friend. You always have been, but I never…we didn't…hell, man, we've never even kissed."

"I'd guessed about you and Sandy, and, when you were in college, there was another woman I wondered about."

"You had reason."

"But I told myself that I was being stupid. Not you, not my old friend, Judy. I didn't think you could be a…"

"Go ahead and say it, a lesbian."

Brad turned away, embarrassed by the very word. "I don't even want to think it."

"You just paid an unannounced visit to my lover and me in our bedroom. Why the hell can't you say it?"

"I didn't like seeing it, either," he hissed.

"Brad, what do you want me to say?"

"I want you to tell me it was a mistake! I want you to tell me that it's really me you want."

"Then you want me to lie."

There were tears in his eyes. "Yes."

"I don't lie to you, Brad. That's part of our friendship."

"Then why didn't you tell me you liked women?"

"You didn't ask."

"Didn't you have any idea how I felt for you?"

Judy pushed back her disheveled hair. "No... maybe...I don't know."

"Jesus, I'm thirty-five years old. When was the last time you knew me to date a woman steady?"

"I don't recall. I didn't really think about it."

Brad threw his fencing gloves on the dashboard. "What did you suppose was going on?"

"I thought, maybe, you just wanted to be alone. You do have to be married to ranching life to live the way we do. Or I thought..."

"What?"

"I thought, maybe...hell, if it could be true for me, it could be true for you. Your trips to Dallas...I thought, maybe, you preferred..."

"I ain't no fucking queer," Brad yelled, his face inches from Judy's.

"Well I am!"

Brad was on her before Judy had time to think. His mouth crushed against hers in a parody of a kiss that left her lips bleeding and her heart aching with betrayal. His hands tore at her shirt, and he bruised her breast as his fingers dug into the flesh. There was little room to move as Judy fought to push him away. Her hand fell, accidently, on a can of WD-40. Using the weapon of opportunity, she threw all her strength into a single blow to the side of Brad's head.

Unasked, a thought came from a part of Judy's brain where humor was a habit. A thousand and one uses, Judy thought as she dropped the can. Judy fought with hysterical laughter as Brad slumped, and she pushed him away. She was out the door and running across the pasture in an instant.

Brad didn't follow. When she was a relatively safe distance, she looked back, concerned at how badly she had hurt her friend. She saw Brad standing beside the pickup. In the distance, she could see a trickle of blood down the side of his face, and she was sure he was shaking with uncontrollable sobs.

"Brad," Judy called.

Her friend, her oldest friend, jumped into his pickup and drove away, leaving Judy alone in the pasture. Judy dropped to the ground and held her arms tightly to her sides, trying to control the shaking.

She didn't lie in the dust for long. Survival is a habit that's hard to break. Brad was the only one who knew where she was, and she didn't expect him to return. The only way home was on her own two legs. Judy began the three-mile walk back to her vehicle.

It wasn't long before she regretted the haste that had caused her to pull her boots onto sockless feet. She continued to walk as the blisters formed, and she continued to walk as the blisters burst. Judy was almost grateful. The pain in her feet distracted her from the pain in her heart. Judy was still a mile from the pickup when she spotted Kathleen's Escort, progressing across the pasture at a sedate pace. Using both arms in a windmill wave, Judy attracted Kathleen's attention, and the car, unsuited to the rough terrain, changed course to ease its way toward Judy.

When Kathleen opened the door and stepped out to hold her lover, both dogs bailed out of the car and whined and barked at their mistresses' feet. Judy could feel the heat of her lover's anger as Kathleen lightly touched Judy's bruised lips and raised the torn cloth of Judy's shirt to see the darkening fingerprints on her lover's breasts.

"The bastard! He hurt you," Kathleen said, tears of frustration and anger in her eyes.

"I guess we're even, 'cause I sure as hell hurt him," Judy said.

Judy dissolved into tears and took welcome refuge in her lover's arms.

They went home. The horses were late getting fed that morning, but they were fed. Life goes on.

Chapter Sixteen

The noise tore through the darkness like a knife through the heart. Judy groped toward the nightstand, knocking the blaring alarm onto its back before she finally found the button that strangled the clock into silence.

She'd done it all before. It was gathering day again.

This time it was different…better. Kathleen curled against her, all warm and comforting. Judy thought gratefully of the invention of the snooze button as she let herself drift back into the cocoon of their bed. Judy had actually slept well. The anxiety, which usually kept her sleepless and watchful in the darkness before the big day, was inexplicably eased by the presence of Kathleen in both her life and her bed. Kathleen made most everything better, or at least bearable.

Kathleen eased but couldn't eliminate the pain Judy felt at her estrangement from Brad. Remembering her lifelong friend and his ongoing anger destroyed Judy's last comfortable moments of sleepiness. Brad refused to speak to her or even acknowledge her existence since that ill-fated day when he had chosen to face the truth. It had been with great apprehension that Judy called the Kenton home to tell them of the workday she had planned, to gather and separate the cows and calves. She had considered not including them in the day's activity, but Judy couldn't remember a time when the Proctors and the Kentons hadn't worked side by side. Continuing that tradition was worth the risk of rejection.

Martha Kenton sounded relieved when she heard Judy's voice.

"What did you and Brad fight about?" Martha asked.

"Life," Judy answered.

"Don't tell me if you don't want to, but you two better mend your fences. We may not be blood kin, but we're family, and don't you forget it, Judy Proctor."

An unseen hand tightened on Judy's throat. "I know, Martha, but this is going to take some time."

A spasm of static filled the telephone line during an anxious silence.

"Judy," Martha said, still gathering courage.

"Yes?"

"Did my boy finally ask you to marry him?"

Judy cleared her throat. "Sort of."

"What'd you tell him?"

"No."

The anxious silence returned. "Are you sure about this, Judy?"

"Yes, Martha. I love Brad. I love you all, but I got no business marrying Brad or anybody for that matter."

"I'd always hoped…"

"I'm sorry, but it just won't be."

Martha sighed so deeply that Judy imagined the breath brushing past her face over the telephone line. The older woman was worried, anxious, and little bit put out, but she'd be there. Judy knew that the man and woman who were second parents to her would help with the gathering. She wondered about Brad. It was a question that had plagued her for days. The thought of a final ending to their friendship left Judy's stomach in a painful knot, and her heart aching.

Thank God for Kathleen's arms…for Kathleen's welcoming warmth and patient ear.

"Time to get up," Judy said as she rolled to her side. She brushed her lips against Kathleen's sleeping face.

"No," Kathleen mumbled. A smile peeked through her befuddled features. "Five more minutes, Mom."

Judy laughed. "You got 'em, but you'd better be ready to snort caffeine when I return with coffee."

Routine helped ease Judy's concerns about Brad. She checked the beans in the Crock-Pot and started the coffee maker. A breakfast of peanut butter and toast was soon ready, and Judy munched on hers as she poured coffee. Kathleen stretched luxuriantly as Judy returned to the bedroom, a coffee cup in each hand, and a bread plate holding Kathleen's breakfast balanced atop one.

"If I have to wake up at an ungodly hour, this is the way to do it," Kathleen said.

Judy set the cups and plate on the nightstand and crawled back under the covers. Both women lounged comfortably as they drank their coffee. Kathleen studied Judy, concern in her eyes.

"You think Brad will come today?" Kathleen asked.

"Who knows?" A flicker of pain crossed Judy's face. "I hope so."

Kathleen placed her hand over Judy's.

"I'm so sorry, baby."

"Don't be sorry, it's not your fault."

"But it is."

"Why?"

Kathleen laughed dryly. "Because Brad can't handle the fact that you love a woman, and I'm the woman you love."

Judy grasped the front of Kathleen's t-shirt and pulled her close. Judy kissed Kathleen with an intensity and depth that couldn't be mistaken for anything but honesty.

"That's Brad's problem," Judy said.

"Yeah," Kathleen whispered as her arms engulfed Judy and pulled her lover into another kiss.

Both women jumped as the alarm buzzed for the third time. Judy hit the button and looked at the time.

"Jimminy! We better get going," she said.

Within minutes, both women were dressed. After they locked the dogs in the shed (not even Somegood was welcome when working young calves), Judy made mental note that she would have to change her early morning gathering schedule, now that Kathleen was with her. The sun was already sending bold rays of light across the landscape as Judy unlocked the tack room, so that they could retrieve the bridles and catch the horses. Judy had barely finished saddling Jackson, when she heard the Kenton pickup and trailer rattle into the yard. Judy fought to steady her breathing when she spotted two horses in the trailer. As the pickup drew closer, she detected the distinctive outline of Brad's well-weathered Stetson.

Harold Kenton was driving, and he stopped well away from where the two women were working. Brad's father stepped out of the pickup and walked toward Judy and Kathleen.

The three of them exchanged morning greetings. Harold's cheerfulness was strained.

"Glad you and Brad could make it, but I'm afraid we're running a little slow," Judy said.

Harold watched as Kathleen finished fastening the back cinch on Big Tom.

"I see Judy let you graduate off of Old Buck," Harold observed.

"Once I'm in the saddle, Big Tom and I get along great," Kathleen answered.

Judy laughed. "First time she rode him, I thought I was going to have to buy climbing gear, just so she could mount."

Harold's habitual smile deepened the weathered creases in his face. "Your dad would be pleased to see Tom getting the exercise."

Judy blinked back the sting of tears. Her emotions were on edge.

"Yeah, he would," Judy said as she pretended to retighten her front cinch. She swallowed hard. "Why doesn't Brad come on over?"

"He ain't feeling too well," Harold answered.

"Tell him I'm awful pleased he came," Judy said.

"Yeah." Harold dug in the ground with the toe of his boot. "We going to start gathering in the southeast pasture?"

"Yes."

"We'll meet you there."

As Harold turned to leave, Judy waved hopefully at the silhouette of Brad in the pickup. He was looking away, studying something that wasn't there.

"You going to make it through today?" Kathleen asked as the Kenton pickup and trailer pulled away.

"Reckon I'll have to," Judy answered.

Nothing went wrong that day. The cows and calves gathered like it was something they wanted to do. As inexperienced as she was, Kathleen knew that was nothing short of a miracle. She also knew that on this day, a miracle was needed. The tension was so thick between Judy and Brad that even the two hands from the Bar D could feel it. Kathleen overheard one of them say something about a lovers' quarrel.

The tension was there, but the job was still done. In an unspoken collusion, Kathleen and Harold cooperated in keeping Judy and Brad apart. As the calves were separated from the cows, Harold and Kathleen ran the gates in the alley, a job usually performed by Brad, while Judy worked the cattle and signaled which pens would hold the individual animals. There were three basic pens, a cow pen, a calf pen, and a cull pen. Harold ran the gate to the hazardous cow pen, where thousand pound cows could be awesome, while Kathleen watched for calves. The culled cows, those that would make the trip to the auction, were sent to the end of the alley. There, the Bar D hands moved them down another alley and into a separate pen. During this process, Brad prepared the propane branding fire and the tools needed to castrate and dehorn the calves.

Once the cows were separated from the calves, Brad and the Bar D hands drove the cows back to pasture, while Judy, Harold, and Kathleen resorted the calves into bulls and heifers. Judy always preferred to work the bulls first. Castration made the whole process much more traumatic for both cattle and hands. She preferred to finish that job before weariness made the workers' movements heavy and tempers short. It was a trick she had learned from her father.

Although she had been warned about what to expect, Kathleen felt nauseous as the first bull went through the branding chute. Somegood and Useless, recently released from the shed, had a very different reaction. Both dogs sat expectantly near the bucket where the workers tossed the fresh mountain oysters as they were removed from the bawling calves. Any testicle that missed the bucket was the immediate property of the quicker of the two dogs. Kathleen was soon too busy to waste thought on the bloody process in the branding chute. She was assigned the exhausting task of keeping fresh cattle shoved up the narrow alley so that there was always another one ready to go when the workers at the chute finished with the last animal. It was the task requiring the least skill and involving the least danger, but it was demanding. She was constantly climbing up and down the small walkway that ran along the alley, using the electric hotshot or a whip to push the cattle forward. Soon, she was as covered in sweat and dirt as any of the seasoned cowboys.

"Looks like you found yourself a pretty good hand," commented one of the Bar D hands to Judy as they released an animal from the chute.

"Damn right," Judy answered.

"And she looks a helluva lot better than the boys at our place," he added.

Judy laughed as she hit the hydraulic control that closed the sides of the chute on the next calf.

They were half way through the heifers when the Kenton's Buick pulled up to the house. Every cowhand watched Martha Kenton's movements, as she made frequent trips from car to house, carrying pies and vegetables. Stomachs rumbled as the workers recalled

Martha Kenton's cooking. The others expected their reaction, but Kathleen was surprised at her sudden ravenousness. She didn't think she had ever been so hungry, or tired, in her life.

Judy paused and walked toward her lover.

"Why don't you go to the house and help Martha?" Judy said.

"I'm fine," Kathleen answered, irritated. The exhausted droop of her shoulders contradicted her words.

Judy lowered her voice, ensuring that the others couldn't hear over the bedlam of the working pen. "Baby, you're new to this, and you wouldn't believe how well you're doing. I'm so proud of you I could bust, but too much time in the sun and dirt can make you sicker than you'd ever want to be. Besides, the crew will appreciate you all the more if you make sure dinner is ready as soon as we finish. There's too much for Martha to do alone."

Kathleen rested her hotshot against the side of the alley. "You're not just saying this to protect me?"

"No, baby, I'm not." Judy looked away, afraid the other workers could see what she was feeling. She studied the ground intently. "God, you're beautiful."

Kathleen laughed as she rubbed her work glove over her face, leaving a streak in the dirt. "You're kidding."

Judy looked at her lover. For a second, she let the full depth of her emotions flash through her eyes. It was all the proof Kathleen needed.

"They're certainly giving you an initiation, today," Martha said as Kathleen entered the kitchen.

"I'm loving it," Kathleen answered.

"Don't you work too hard. It takes time to

harden to this life."

Kathleen retrieved the bedraggled bar of Lava soap from under the sink. The smoothness of freshly cleaned skin appeared on her hands, while little, dirty rivulets ran down the sink. Kathleen felt an itch on the back of her neck and turned to see Martha Kenton studying her openly.

"It's good that Judy's finally got some company," Martha said.

"I'm happy she's let me stay," Kathleen answered. She finished drying her hands and turned to pour cornbread batter into a dish.

"Aren't you here to do an article?"

"Yes."

"Judy will be sad when it's done."

"I submitted that article some time ago. Judy's just letting me stay around while I work on my novel."

"Oh, I see." Martha busied herself retrieving bowls and plates from the cabinet. "You have any idea what Brad and Judy fought about?"

Kathleen wished she was still out struggling in the sun. "Yes."

"Would you mind telling me?"

Kathleen gazed directly at the older woman. "Yes, I would mind. If you want to know, you need to ask Brad or Judy."

"I already have," Martha answered, disgusted.

Martha's movements were frenzied as she cut pies and made fresh, brewed tea. The woman was obviously upset and directing her emotional energy toward her work. A strained silence filled the air of the homey kitchen. A twinge of regret made Kathleen wonder if there couldn't have been a better answer to Martha's question. She could think of none. The only alternative to the evasion she had used was direct honesty. Kathleen didn't like to imagine Martha Kenton's reaction if she had told her, "Brad's angry because I'm Judy's lover." The solution would cause more pain than the problem.

The tension remained thick between Martha and Kathleen. Kathleen was relieved when the cowhands retreated from the corrals to the house, for their belated lunch.

There was a grim set to Judy's mouth, as she walked into the kitchen. She retrieved the work-worn bar of Lava soap and hand towels from a drawer.

"Did it go well?" Martha asked.

"Couldn't hope for better," Judy answered, the tone of her voice belying the positive words.

Judy went back outside, taking the soap and towels to where the workers waited beside the backyard water hydrant. Martha and Kathleen stepped to the window so they could better see the workers.

"Wonder what's wrong with Judy?" Martha said.

They studied the cowhands as they took turns washing the day's filth from face and hands. Kathleen and Martha's gazes met as they both arrived at the same realization.

"Brad's not there." Kathleen said.

"That's strange. He's usually the first in line when a meal's waiting." Martha stepped back and looked out another window to where the vehicles were parked. "Our pickup's gone."

Both women stepped back from the window as Harold Kenton, the first to finish washing, walked into the kitchen.

"I'll be riding home with you," he said to his wife.

"Where's Brad?" she asked.

"He wasn't feeling well so he went on home," Harold answered.

Judy said nothing as she entered the kitchen. She turned her back to the others, as she opened a cabinet, pretending to look for plates that were already on the table. Kathleen stepped to her side. From that angle she could see the silvery glisten of tears in her lover's eyes. Kathleen grasped Judy's arm in a brief squeeze. She willed comfort to her lover.

"Looks like you two have everything under control," Judy said with forced cheerfulness.

"Beans are ready and cornbread's done," Martha answered.

Judy turned abruptly and walked across the kitchen. Without warning she placed her arms around Martha's neck and gave her second mother a bone cracking hug.

"Thanks for being here and thanks for all the help," Judy said.

Kathleen could now see the glisten of tears reflected in Martha's eyes.

"Damn it, girl. Of course we're here. We love you."

Judy released Martha and stepped to Harold. He lifted her off the ground as he returned the bear hug.

"Whatever it is, he'll get over it," Harold said.

Judy looked at him long and hard. "Harold, this is something Brad may not forgive. If…if you knew, you might not either."

Martha stepped to Judy's side. "You're family, Judy girl. We could no more push you out of our lives than we could willingly cut off a hand or a finger."

Judy placed a hand on each of the Kentons'

shoulders.

"Martha, Harold, hang around after the Bar D boys go home."

"Why?" Harold asked.

Judy's gaze locked with Kathleen's. Kathleen felt an anxious lump in her throat.

"I got something to tell you."

The kitchen door opened and the Bar D hands entered.

"Lordie, is that cornbread I smell?" one man asked.

"Feed me fast, before I blow plumb away," the other added. Judy moved close to Kathleen's side, and the man walked to where he could place an arm around each of their shoulders.

"Slim, we got it made today," he said to his companion. "Good food and the company of two beautiful ladies."

"Watch yourself, Chub," the other responded. "Miss Judy here keeps that castrating knife sharp."

"And the beans well-cooked with just a taste of jalapeño," Judy countered. "Let's eat."

❧❧❧❧

Judy painted like a madwoman. Now and again, Kathleen would look into the study that also served as Judy's art studio when she was so inclined to drag out easel and canvas. The painting had none of the gentle color and peacefulness of Judy's other renditions of life on the range. There was a darkness to it, a ragged edged power, and angry beauty. Judy hadn't even bothered with the charcoal sketch to rough out her idea before putting paint to canvas. She had too much passion and pain invested in the raw paint.

Neither woman had slept well the night before, despite the physical exhaustion from shipping day. Kathleen had stayed close as Judy confessed to Martha and Walter the real reason why she could never marry their son. Even when Kathleen saw the flash of hatred Walter couldn't keep from his eyes as he looked Kathleen's direction, she stayed. Judy needed her.

As coming out sessions went, it could have been worse. The older couple listened in silence. There was a crackle of tension in the air, and Judy's voice had a slight tremble of fear…one uncommon for the normally courageous woman.

"What would your daddy say?" was Walter's only question to break his tight-lipped silence.

"Walter, he knew." Judy responded. "He…he got used to the idea."

Once the truth was out, there were more painful silences than words. After a while, the older couple just stood, gathered their things, and left. Walter didn't even say goodbye, and there were tears in her eyes as Martha gave Judy a long farewell hug. Neither even looked at Kathleen nor spoke to her.

"We need time to think," Martha said, glancing back at Judy before she closed the back door.

Kathleen had held Judy tightly that night. She'd felt her lover tense and sleepless beside her. Judy rose with the sun the next morning, making short work of morning chores, feeding horses and caring for dogs. Kathleen made coffee and practiced her new found biscuit making skills. When Judy returned to the house, she went straight to the study, barely stopping for a kiss and a long, slow embrace.

A storm grew on the canvas. Dark clouds and

a haze of rain almost hid the ranch house, while lightning flashed across the sky. Horses huddled against the fence, butts to the storm and heads down. It was hauntingly beautiful. Judy didn't notice when Kathleen put hot coffee with a biscuit and jelly on the desk beside the easel. Three hours later, her frenzy of painting was nearly done, and the coffee stood cold and untouched.

When Judy finished, she wiped paint from her hands on an old rag, and left the study for the kitchen where Kathleen sat at the table, trying unsuccessfully to concentrate on a half-written chapter on the computer. Judy planted a quick kiss on her lover's head before taking a clean cup from the cabinet and pouring fresh coffee. She looked tired, but the haunted look in her eyes was eased. She took a biscuit from a bowl, slathering it with butter and honey, before sitting at the table.

"You're getting good at biscuits," Judy said.

"Don't tell my grandmother. She was always disappointed that I preferred to buy my tortillas." There was silence as Judy ate and drank greedily. "You okay?" Kathleen asked.

Judy took Kathleen's hand, giving her lover a sad smile. "No, but I will be. Martha and Walter will come around. They're family and love runs deep."

"What about Brad?"

Judy's expression tightened. "Bastard better come around. Who else is he going to get to help pull a well?"

Chapter Seventeen

The letter fluttered in the breeze from the open window. Kathleen held it, half forgotten and nearly slipping from her grasp, as she looked absently out the window at the pasture across the road. Her computer still hummed on the desk before her, the cursor blinking, completely forgotten. In the peace of Judy's country home, Kathleen's novel was progressing well, but not today. Today, her mind was too occupied with other concerns.

It was time for a decision. The letter, forwarded from her Colorado Springs address, robbed Kathleen of the option of procrastination.

She was intrigued by Judy Proctor from the first moment the ranch woman walked into the *Gazette* office. Before their first lunch was finished, Kathleen knew she wanted the woman. Judy oozed strength and peace, and Kathleen loved the young/old look of Judy's weathered face. The simple grace of the rancher's well-muscled body distracted Kathleen from the meal more than the conversation. The fantasies began early. On the drive back to the newspaper office, Kathleen was already imagining her first night on the ranch, but she didn't know. She was not sure if Judy was gay, or simply a strong and independent woman who was butch because of circumstance, instead of sexual preference. Then there was Judy's reserve, and Kathleen was not accustomed to being the initiator.

With her long legs, warm brown eyes, and soft hair, she never worried about starting a relationship. They always came to her.

Then, and for a long time afterward, Kathleen anticipated Judy as a pleasant and passing sexual experience. She had not planned on losing her heart.

The roar of the tractor distracted Kathleen. From the window, she could see Judy pull the tractor around the side of the house to clear the culvert on the crossover from the county road to the pasture, across from the house. Last big rain, the water had backed up leaving a small lake across the road and into the farmyard, nearly to the house. As Kathleen watched, Judy used the front-end loader to move the silt that had collected at the opening to the corrugated iron pipe. The work was tedious, scooping the earth without damaging road or culvert.

Watching Judy's skilled efforts brought Kathleen more joy than she expected. A memory of the pleasures they had shared the night before flashed through Kathleen's thoughts, and she felt her breathing quicken.

Kathleen had not planned on losing her heart, but lose it she did. God how that complicated life. Her grasp on the nearly forgotten letter tightened, as she raised it to read the words once again.

The article was a dream assignment from a well-paid market. When she sent the query months earlier, Kathleen had barely dared to hope for its success.

During her stay with Judy, Kathleen had received requests for other articles, but they were all on subjects she had already researched and photographed. The simple matter of writing new articles had posed no conflict between her work and her desire to stay on at the ranch.

Kathleen tossed the letter on top of her computer. This was different.

The tractor stopped in mid scoop. Kathleen watched as Judy looked up from her work and down the road. As she redirected her concentration, Kathleen could hear a pickup approaching. She watched from her limited view through the window, as the pickup drew closer. Not dropping speed, the pickup roared past the house like a lightning visit from a science fiction fantasy.

Brad's pickup.

Judy sat behind the wheel of the patiently waiting tractor. Kathleen watched as her lover backed the tractor to level ground and dismounted from the cab to lean against the tractor wheel and stare longingly at the cloud of dust left by the man who was once her friend.

There was an ache in Kathleen's chest to match the one she knew was tightening around Judy's heart. For the moment, Kathleen forgot about her need to make a decision. She saved the half-written chapter on the computer screen and then shut down the machine. Kathleen was already developing the habits of the country. Before leaving the house, she donned the John Deere ball cap she had appropriated as her own. Judy wouldn't let her work in the sun without a hat.

"How's it going?" Kathleen asked as she stepped beside her lover.

There was a hint of pain in Judy's smile, and Kathleen found her arms enclosing her lover in a desire to ease that pain.

"I'll have this little job done soon," Judy answered, her lips brushing against Kathleen's neck.

"Can I help?"

"I thought you were writing this afternoon. I don't want you to leave your book."

Kathleen shrugged. "The brain's on strike."

"I'm sorry."

"And I'm sorry Brad gave you the cold shoulder," Kathleen said.

The pained expression returned to Judy's face as she looked back down the road. "It's to be expected. I guess I always knew how he'd react, and that's why I never told him I was gay."

"It goes with the life, babe."

"I know, but it's a bitch, ain't it?" Judy pulled off her work gloves and leaned back from her lover as she stuffed them in her back pocket. "Trouble is, now I can see how bad it was for me to live a lie all these years."

"How's that?"

"I've been friends with Brad all my life, and I've been actively gay since college."

"So?"

"So, for the past fourteen years, I've been wasting my time on a friendship with someone who liked me just because he thought I was something I wasn't."

"At least Martha and Harold haven't turned you out," Kathleen said.

"Martha hasn't anyway. Harold, hell, Harold hasn't figured out what he thinks."

Kathleen searched for comforting words. She could find none.

"You know what?" Kathleen finally asked.

"What?"

"I have a sudden need to be around family."

Judy's eyes widened in surprise. "Your folks in

Arizona? Mercy, Kathleen, do you...do you want me to go with you?"

Kathleen laughed and then paused in thought. "You know, I really would love for you to meet my parents, but that's not what I meant."

"What then?"

"I didn't mean family, I meant family."

Judy laughed. "Sorry, I'm not used to thinking that way."

"Do you think we could get away for a couple of days and go to Colorado Springs, or even Denver? I know some good places there."

"Maybe, although it was always Brad I called to check cattle and wells when I was gone. We don't have to go all the way to Colorado. We can go out tonight."

"In Dulson County!"

Judy's laughter indicated that she, too, thought the idea shocking. "No, in Amarillo. It's only an hour and a half away."

"Do they have any bars?"

"Sure. Did you think I was the only gay or lesbian in the whole Panhandle?"

"I didn't really think about it." Kathleen shook her head, trying to find a niche for this new side to her lover. "You actually go to the bars?"

"Some, but not often. I'm not one for the casual sex stuff."

Kathleen blushed.

Judy turned serious. "I've never asked, and I never will if you don't want me to."

"Asked what?"

A sideways look told Kathleen that Judy knew she was avoiding the issue. "The same question every lover wants to ask at some point in time."

"What?" Kathleen demanded.

"How many women you've had."

Kathleen turned a deeper shade of red. She took Judy's hand and pulled her toward the house.

"This is a conversation I'd rather have in the house, preferably in bed."

"Lord, is the answer that bad?" Judy asked, only half teasing.

Kathleen drug Judy through the house and into their bedroom, where they removed enough of their clothing to lay comfortably on the bed. At first, Judy welcomed the demands of Kathleen's lips, but she was not to be distracted. Judy pointedly removed Kathleen's hand from her own breast and kissed the palm of a hand that was just developing the calluses of hard work.

"You're not going to get off the hook that easily," Judy said and then leaned against the headboard, her arms crossed against her chest. "How many women have you had?"

Kathleen sighed. "I thought you said you wouldn't ask if I didn't want to answer."

"I lied."

"Oh God." She looked unhappily at her lover. "Judy, I don't really know."

Judy laughed. Her amusement had an edge to it. "You've got to be kidding."

"Oh come on, Judy. You're one of the few lesbians I know who managed to avoid the slut puppy stage." Kathleen sat up to rest against the headboard. "Most of my experience came after I went to college. I've told you about Claudine, in high school. We didn't do much, but it answered a whole lot of questions I had about myself. When I went off to school, it was like the whole world opened up for me. Benito...."

"Your pain-in-the-ass brother?"

"Yeah. Anyway, Benito was no longer there to torment me, and I learned that I really could open up to people. One of the upper classwomen spotted me as family, long before I knew that use of the term. She quickly introduced me to the gay lifestyle, including the bars." Kathleen took a drink from the glass of water left on the nightstand. "At the time, I just thought it was fun. I was like a kid just introduced to candy."

"Did you get a belly ache?" Judy asked, her voice was husky with emotion.

Kathleen laughed, but there were tears at the edge of the laughter. "Big time. I think it screwed me up for a long time about what it meant to love someone." The tears sparkled at the edge of her eyes as she looked directly at Judy. "I pray to God it hasn't screwed me up forever."

Judy pulled her lover close, kissing her gently, more with love than passion.

"You've given me more happiness than anyone has ever done before. You know when I hurt before I even realize it, and you're finally getting where you'll let me see your pain. Somebody who's screwed up couldn't do that, now could she?"

Kathleen buried her face between Judy's breasts, thinking painfully of the letter and the decision she now faced.

"I hope not, baby. I hope not."

Judy laughed as she stroked Kathleen's braided hair. "I should have known."

"Known what?"

"I knew you were good in bed, but I thought it was just natural talent."

Kathleen blushed. "I'm sorry, Judy, but I can't take back the life I've lived."

Judy held her close. "We all have history. I fell in love with you for the person you are. You have no reason to apologize. Besides, would you really want to take back your life?"

There was a momentary pause for thought, before Kathleen answered. "No."

"Me either. I'll take the hand I'm dealt and keep on playing."

"Amen."

A reluctant expression of concern marred Judy's face.

"What is it?" Kathleen asked.

"Have you ever been…?" Judy paused.

Kathleen's face set in an expression of resolve. "AIDS tested?"

"Yes."

"Of course. Even though it's been a lot of years since I've been that sexually irresponsible…"

Judy smiled. "A slut puppy."

Kathleen returned the smile shyly. "Yeah. Anyway, I still try to go in once a year for an AIDS test."

"I've gone too," Judy said.

"You? Why?"

"I may not have gained slut puppy status, but I want to be safe."

"We're really in a low risk group, you know?"

"Low risk, but not no risk."

A laugh of pure relief accented Kathleen's movements as she stretched full-length on the bed. "God, you don't know how much I've dreaded this conversation. I'm glad it's over."

Judy moved to where her body measured along her lover's. "Why did you dread it?"

Kathleen touched her lover's face. "Because I thought you might send me packing."

"You're not going to get rid of me that easy," Judy whispered against Kathleen's ear. Kathleen shivered in anticipation.

The remainder of the afternoon could best be described as pleasant, extremely pleasant. When they finally left their bed so they could shower and consume a quick meal, it was almost too late for their trip to Amarillo.

Chapter Eighteen

The bartender was one gorgeous cross-dresser. It wasn't until he spoke that Kathleen realized he was male.

"Hey girlfriend. Long time no see," he said as Judy leaned against the bar.

"I've had better things to do," Judy yelled over the Garth Brooks number blaring through the sound system.

The bartender looked Kathleen over from end to end and back again. "I can see," he said. "Now, what'll you have?"

"How about two of your bitching margaritas?"

"Oh, yeass," he answered as he performed a quick twirl to the music.

Kathleen leaned close against Judy's back, her arm around her lover's waist, and spoke directly into Judy's ear. "Tell me I'm not dreaming. Is this really the Texas Panhandle?"

Judy laughed and turned to give her lover a quick kiss. It felt good, expressing her affection for Kathleen where all could see. "Trust me, you're standing right in the middle of the cattle feeding capital of the world. What did you think gays and lesbians did out here?"

"Moved to California."

"Or Colorado," Judy added.

Kathleen looked around the crowded room. "This doesn't seem like the kind of place you'd go to," she said.

"I prefer it during the week. It's a lot quieter, and I could always find a friend to talk to or somebody wanting to play pool."

"Ever have anyone pick you up?"

Judy blushed. "Once."

"How'd it go?"

"Disaster."

As they waited for their drinks, Kathleen felt the beat of the music throb through the floor and her boots to make the bottoms of her feet tingle. She closed her eyes and placed her arms around Judy as they both swayed ever so slightly to the beat. Returning, was some of the old excitement that had drawn Kathleen to the bars, made better with Judy there beside her. There had been pleasure in the music, laughter, and the simple lust of her barhopping days, but with an emptiness to it all. Now, the pounding of music and the thrill of watching dancers animate the very air around them felt like what it should be, dessert for something more substantial.

The drinks arrived and Kathleen took a sip. The bartender did make bitching margaritas, the best she'd ever tasted. There was even the right amount of salt around the rim to accent the drink without overpowering it.

On a Saturday night, there were no empty tables to be found. They left the bar and found a small space near the pool table, where they could rest their drinks on a shelf attached to the wall. The place was smaller than most of the gay bars Kathleen had frequented, but she liked the feel of it. Kathleen had grown to love the habitual courtesy and openness of the people of the Panhandle, and the feeling extended into the bar.

Before meeting Judy, Kathleen avoided the country bars. Now, she found her feet tapping in anticipation of using her newfound dancing skills. Judy, as always, was sensitive to Kathleen's mood.

"Want to dance?" Judy asked.

In answer, Kathleen took her lover's hand and half drug her onto the dance floor. Dance after dance they moved together, enjoying the magical harmony they had developed in the kitchen of Judy's home.

They danced the two-step. They danced the waltz. As the evening progressed, the simple steps were complicated by new variations that grew out of their own creativity and a looseness nurtured by tequila. They danced until sweat matted hair to heads and their feet burned within their boots, and then they danced some more. Somewhere during the whirl of the evening, Judy introduced Kathleen to others she knew who were making their own way onto the dance floor. One woman, tall with short, dark hair and determination in her eyes, cut in. She stole Kathleen away for half a number, but Judy reclaimed her lover before the dance ended. Kathleen saw a flash of challenge in the dark-haired woman's eyes. Kathleen greeted Judy with a long, slow kiss, making it clear whose company she chose. The woman disappeared somewhere in the crowd. Neither Judy nor Kathleen saw her again.

Together they laughed at everything and at nothing. They twirled until they were dizzy and then leaned against the wall, claiming their half-forgotten drinks as they held each other close, recuperating for yet another dance.

It was two a.m. by the time they stumbled to their motel room (within walking distance of the bar), trying to contain their giggles in consideration of the other guests. They showered together and collapsed into bed, too exhausted to complete the lovemaking they initiated. They lay intertwined, drifting into sleep.

"Tonight was fantastic," Judy mumbled against her lover's neck.

"Um-hum," Kathleen responded.

"It's been an eventful day."

"Yes, my love. Now go to sleep."

Judy snuggled closer. "Kathleen?"

"Yes, love."

"I forgot to ask. What was your letter this morning?"

Kathleen's mind snapped back to wakefulness. Feeling her lover tense, Judy fought through the sleepiness and raised on one elbow so that she could look into Kathleen's face.

"What is it?" she asked.

"It's an article assignment," Kathleen answered, reluctant.

Judy's throat tightened. "You've got to go?"

There was strain in Kathleen's voice. "Yes."

"Right now."

"No, I have a couple of months before the deadline."

"Can you stay for Pioneer Days?" Judy asked.

"Wouldn't miss it."

Judy touched Kathleen's face lightly with her fingers. "The assignment won't last forever, lover."

"There'll be others."

"And they won't last forever, either. Between times, you have to live someplace."

"Yes, I do."

With as much depth of feeling as she had ever known, Judy spoke. "Live with me," she said.

Judy's emotion was reflected in Kathleen's gaze. "We'll see," Kathleen said.

For now, it was enough for Judy that she could hope.

They slept, totally exhausted, in each other's arms.

Chapter Nineteen

The dance was unlike anything Kathleen had ever seen before, but then, the same could be said of the whole weekend. Nothing Judy could have said would have prepared Kathleen for the full reality of Pioneer Days. It was a giant of an old-fashioned country rodeo/parade/barbecue/dance…the kind of event only country folks could create. The tradition started from the days when most of the year was filled with loneliness and hard work, among folks whose nearest neighbor was a half day's ride away. Their entire social life was packed into the occasional celebration where one ranch or community would host people from a two or three county area, in whatever excuse they could find for a full-scale celebration. In the days of cars, cell phones, and Internet, the tradition remained and continued to prove that country folk know just about all there is to know about having fun.

As they pulled into the overcrowded parking lot, surrounding the county bull barn, they could hear the thunder of the country-western band. As they walked closer, Kathleen swore she could hear the sheet metal on the barn rattle from the music.

Both women were exhausted but happy. As a local, Judy was naturally one of the thousands of hosts the community needed to pull off an event that, for three days, nearly tripled the town's population. Kathleen was drafted into sharing the task. They'd shucked corn at six in the morning for the sweet corn feed, and sold soft drinks and hot dogs through two rodeos. Kathleen watched proudly as Judy served as flagman for the afternoon team roping, but she thought the best may very well have been the fire.

Kathleen originally thought Judy was crazy to keep them up until two a.m. when they were both footsore and tired from duty in the concession stand. That was before she saw the fire.

A barbecue for ten thousand people required one helluva pit. The fire had to be started in the middle of the night, for the coals to be ready for the meat to be placed in the pit and slow cooked. Like most of the tenderfoots, Kathleen stood expectantly, perhaps ten yards from the hundred-yard long, seven-foot tall stack of wood that began four feet below the ground. As men lit the flares to throw on the diesel and gasoline treated wood, Judy not too gently took Kathleen by the arm and pulled her lover back another ten yards. If she hadn't, Kathleen would have lost her eyebrows.

It wasn't a fire. It was an inferno.

Kathleen would never forget the sound as the fire suddenly took voice, calling a deep whoosh that brought campers out of their trailers and a fascinated smile to the face of everyone who watched. In a rush, the fire blew its warm breath past Kathleen. The fire was alive with so much destructive power, controlled, and beautiful.

Neither lover could completely control her need to share the moment. They grasped hands briefly, but no one seemed to notice. The moment called for hand holding among friends as well as lovers.

"God, Judy, you didn't tell me what it would be

like," Kathleen said.

"Would you have understood? Would you have believed?"

Kathleen stared into the flames. "No. It's something you've got to see."

Now, the fire was behind them…an important memory. One dance remained and Pioneer Days would be over. Both Judy and Kathleen were already feeling the loss. The celebration had been a special time for them, an important sharing of a major tradition in Judy's life.

They would enjoy the dance, and then they would go home. After two nights as guests at Deb Monroe's, they looked forward to returning to their own house and their own bed. Despite the exhaustion, there had been all too many moments of unspent passion.

"Next year, we'll rent a motel room," Judy said during one of the rare moments they were alone.

"Sounds good," Kathleen responded.

Kathleen's response sent a note of joy to Judy's heart. She was beginning to hope that Kathleen would stay.

They stopped at the folding table, where two cowboys were handling money with hands more accustomed to catch ropes. Judy paid for their tickets, and each woman paused to have an inked stamp placed on the back of her hand. The stamp would allow them to come and go throughout the evening and the majority of the night, at least until the band or the concrete dance floor gave out, whichever came first.

Judy and Kathleen paused at the edge of the crowd that was gathered in a circle around the huge dance floor. A wave of blue moved before them as a sea of blue-jeaned dancers spun and shuffled. They stood so close that their arms touched, full-length, but they dared not indulge the urge to intertwine their fingers.

"I wish I could dance with you," Kathleen said in a whisper that would have been a yell in any other circumstance.

"Later," Judy answered.

A hand reached from nowhere and gave Judy a friendly thump on the back. Judy and Kathleen turned to see two of the Bar D boys easing through the crowd to their side.

"Hey there, Chub," Judy called.

"Hey Miss Judy, Kathleen. Ain't this more fun then branding?"

"Smells better, too," Kathleen yelled back.

Chub leaned slightly closer to the city woman and sniffed at her hair. "I'll say," he answered.

Kathleen blushed.

"I was just telling Slim here that there was two beautiful women dying to dance, and the only gentlemanly thing for us to do was to go ask," Chub said.

"Sounds good to me," Judy responded.

It was the first dance of many. Soon, their feet ached and their legs burned from the effort of the Texas two-step and the Cotton-eyed Joe, but still they danced. They refreshed themselves from soft drinks in the concession stand, with an occasional visit to the pickup, to top up with a dollop of bourbon from a bottle stashed in the toolbox.

The crowd was huge, and, for a long time, neither Judy nor Kathleen saw Brad or the blue-eyed beauty who was his constant companion.

"Did you see Brad?" Kathleen asked Judy, as

Chub and Slim escorted them to the side for a breather and a drink.

"Sure did."

"Who's he with?"

"Darned if I know."

"She's a knockout." Kathleen smiled.

"Yeah," Judy grinned in return.

During the next dance, Judy made brief eye contact with Brad, and she was amazed to see an answering smile in his eyes. She watched in bits and pieces through the crowd as he maneuvered the blue-eyed woman to a position close to her and Chub. Judy saw Brad bend to speak to his companion, and when she looked again, Brad and the woman were staring in her direction. To Judy's surprise, the blue-eyed woman smiled shyly. When the music stopped, Brad took the woman by the hand and walked purposely toward Judy and Chub.

"Hey, Judy, Chub, I got someone I want you to meet," Brad said. "This is Sally Burton...used to be Sally Cox."

The name triggered a vague memory for Judy. "Nice to meet you, Sally." She searched her memory in greater detail. "Brad, is this the girl you used to write to me about, when we were in college?"

Brad grinned. "The same."

The music started.

"Let's change partners this dance, Chub, old buddy," Brad said.

"Gosh almighty, Brad. Blue eyes like that, I just might drown in them while you're gone."

The two couples began the two-step rhythm. The dance was a little slower, a little quieter than some of the others. They could talk.

"You seem like a different man, Bradley boy. Are you still mad at me?"

A flicker of pain crossed the newfound happiness on his face. "Always will be I suppose, but mostly, I figure you're still my best friend."

Tears teased at the edge of Judy's eyes. "Glad to hear you say that, old buddy."

They danced with the ease of habit. The old magic was back in their combined movements.

"What made you change your mind?" Judy asked.

"After that day…" he blushed hotly, "sorry about what I did, by the way. It's just that I was so damned desperate."

"Take my advice." There was a hint of anger in Judy's voice. "Don't ever get that desperate again or I'll take more to you than a can of WD-40."

Brad touched a slight scar on his forehead. "That's a lesson I won't soon forget."

"Good." For an instant, Judy felt a renewed fear in the pit of her stomach. Part of her knew that, had Brad really wanted to hurt her, she would be lying lost and dead in the middle of a government pasture…or worse still, she would have had to kill her best friend.

"How'd you end up with Sally…Cox, is it?"

"Burton, now."

Judy felt a twinge of apprehension. "She married?"

"Divorced. I'd heard about it, about a year ago. After I finally got it through my thick head that I couldn't have you, I thought I'd call to see if there might still be a flicker of the old flame."

"Was there?"

Brad gave her his best good-old-boy smile. "It's

a burn I can live with."

"I'm happy for you, Brad, and I'm sorry you and I didn't get this cleared up years ago."

The music ended. Brad stepped back and took her hand in both of his.

"There's still years to come."

"Best friends?" Judy asked.

"Best friends," Brad answered.

Judy felt Kathleen at her side. She didn't see her. She just knew her by her familiar aura.

"You okay?" Kathleen asked.

Judy turned to share her happiest smile. "I'm fantastic."

They left soon after. It seemed like the right time to go home.

As soon as they were away from the lights of town, Kathleen moved next to Judy. It was the first time in three days they could touch without fear of observation. The affection they shared made the thirty-minute drive seem brief. They arrived home, both still filled with an energy that overshadowed their weariness.

Judy parked the pickup and ran ahead to the house.

"What's the hurry?" Kathleen called.

"I gotta go—now," Judy answered.

When Judy returned from the bathroom, the radio was playing country hits, and Kathleen was reading the newspaper while sitting at the kitchen table.

"Anything good?" Judy asked.

"Pictures from the rodeo. You're in the background for one."

"Want my autograph?"

"You actually have the energy to pick up a pen?"

Judy took her lover's hand and pulled Kathleen to her feet. "Tired or not, there's one thing we've got to do before we go to bed."

"What?"

"I want to dance with the woman I've wanted in my arms all evening."

Kathleen's smile was softened by a visible outpouring of love. "Same here, my love."

Reba McEntire's golden voice played on the radio, as Kathleen moved comfortably into Judy's arms, and they danced close and slow. It was the perfect end to a perfect day. They stayed together as the song ended, the dance turning into a long, slow kiss, their hands exploring familiar bodies. They were alive in that moment, forgetting any uncertainty of the future.

Chapter Twenty

J udy didn't turn into the yard at her house. She didn't want to be alone.

The day's mail rested on the pickup seat beside her. For the fifth day in a row, there was no letter from Kathleen. The assignment took her to such remote areas of Arizona, that lack of cell signal or Internet access had forced them to resort to good, old-fashioned mail. Worse, just the night before, Judy had tried to call Kathleen's house, on the off chance Kathleen was home from Arizona. She had reached a telephone company recording.

"This number is no longer in service," the electronic voice said.

A cold fear filled Judy's heart. She laid awake half the night, feeling tiny in the bed meant for two. *It's just that she's been away so long that she decided to disconnect the telephone. She hasn't written because she's busy*, Judy assured herself.

Through it all, another voice whispered in her mind. *She hasn't called because she no longer wants me*, said an unwanted thought.

To fight the thought, Judy sought company. She drove purposely toward the Kenton homestead, several miles away. Brad was in Dallas with his new girlfriend, and Harold was probably at the Clayton Cattle Auction. Martha should be home alone.

As she drove into the yard, Judy could see the

older woman working in the garden behind the house. Martha wore the ancient straw hat with the faded yellow ribbon that she called her gardening hat. Judy stopped near the garden and got out of the pickup to lean on the chicken wire fence that fought, uselessly, to keep the rabbits out of Martha's lush garden. Somegood and Useless were moving in random patterns, their noses to the ground as they searched for the scent of those rabbits.

"You come for tomatoes or company?" Martha asked, hardly pausing as she picked green beans.

"Both," Judy answered.

"You've come to the right place."

Judy opened the gate and retrieved a hoe from where it leaned inside the garden shed. She attacked a small stand of weeds near where Martha worked.

"What you hear from, Kathleen?" Martha asked.

Judy worked with grim determination. "Haven't had a letter in nearly a week."

Martha straightened and pushed at the kinks in her back, while she studied Judy closely.

"Don't worry. She'll call or write soon. She may surprise you and show up on your doorstep."

"How can you know?" Judy tried to hide the quaver in her voice.

"Because I saw how she looked at you and you looked at her. Kathleen's too wise a woman to throw that away."

Judy stopped hoeing as Martha went back to picking. She watched the older woman.

"Martha, thank you for taking everything so well...I mean the news about me being..." Judy paused. She knew Martha was not comfortable with the words. "the way I am," she finished lamely.

"You're still the same Judy you always were. We loved you then, and we love you now. I can't say I approve, but it's not my job to judge."

They worked in silence for some minutes. Judy felt better after Martha's comforting words. Twice, Martha raised to speak and then changed her mind. Judy waited patiently. Finally, Martha found the courage.

"There's something I think you should know," Martha said.

Judy stopped hoeing to give the older woman her full attention.

"Yes?"

Martha sighed shakily. "Once, not long after you were born, Harold and your father went to the stock show in Houston, and your mother came over here to stay with me."

"I've never heard this story."

"And most likely never will again, 'specially not around Harold and Brad."

Martha had Judy's interest.

"Go on," Judy encouraged.

"A big snowstorm came up while the men were gone. It didn't last long, but it was pretty scary. We did the best we could to keep the cattle fed and the ice broke so they could drink. You and Brad were both little, and we were afraid to take you out in the cold, so your mother and I took turns staying with you kids, while the other cared for the cattle."

"This sounds interesting."

"I've never told this story before, girl, so you just be quiet and listen."

"Yes ma'am."

"Anyway, one day I got the pickup stuck out in

the Glen pasture. It was well after dark when I finally walked back to the house. When your mother greeted me at the door, her eyes were nearly wild with fear. I was half frozen from the walk, and she yanked me inside and started pulling off my wet clothes. I was still shivering even after a warm bath and a meal. Your mother insisted I get into bed with her so she could get me warm."

"She did?"

"Lordie, yes. Now shut up and listen." Martha wiped the sweat from her face. Judy was surprised to notice that her hand was shaking. "She felt warm and wonderful as we lay there. Nothing happened, girl, you can be sure of that, but I never forgot how it felt, having your mother warm and close." Judy could see the gentleness of the memory on Martha's face. Martha sighed and her voice was soft as she continued. "I loved your mother, child. I don't approve of…well… women with women, but, I think I understand, at least a little."

"Did you and Mama ever…I mean did you…"

"Good lord, no! We were happily married women. A kiss on the cheek now and again. Nothing more." Martha started picking beans again. "I just thought you had a right to know—seeing as how you turned out and all—that I loved your mother." She sighed, gathering courage, "If times had been different or we'd been braver, I could have loved her a whole lot more."

"Thank you, Martha."

Martha hoisted the bag of beans off the ground. "This is more than enough for tonight and tomorrow night. You want to come in for tea?"

Judy replaced the hoe to its spot in the shed.

"Thanks, but no. I want to go home." She whistled for the dogs as she walked toward the pickup.

"You forgot your tomatoes."

"I really wanted the company."

The conversation with Martha greatly eased Judy's heart and mind. With the possible exception of Deb Monroe, Martha Kenton had the best people instincts of anybody Judy knew. Judy's doubts were lessened, but not completely gone. They didn't disappear totally, until Judy topped the hill approaching her house and spotted the truck parked in the yard.

Even in the distance, Judy recognized the distinctive color and shape of the U-Haul. Her anxiety turned to an excitement that increased exponentially, as she drew close enough to discern the two-tone blue of the Ford Escort attached to a hitch at the back of the truck.

Judy called, "Yahoo," and the two dogs barked in response from the back of the pickup. When she accelerated abruptly, the dogs slid off their perches, Somegood from the toolbox and Useless from the spare tire. They scrambled for footing in the pickup bed. Judy rounded the corner into the drive at a dangerous speed and parked at a creative angle beside the U-Haul. She ran through the porch and into the kitchen where she found Kathleen standing at the counter slicing tomatoes, the smell of freshly fried bacon in the air. Despite Kathleen's apparent calm, Judy noticed that her lover handled the knife with shaky hands.

"You're back," Judy said, driven to stating the obvious.

Kathleen wiped her hands on a towel and turned

to face her lover.

"I decided you were right, I have to live somewhere between assignments." Kathleen's voice was hesitant with fear. "Will you let me stay?"

Judy laughed in joy and crossed the kitchen in a single jump. She grasped Kathleen in a hug so hard it made her back pop. At first, the kiss was harsh in intensity and haste. Gradually, the gentleness so basic to their love replaced the intensity. The doubts from their enforced separation evaporated.

When Judy stepped away and took her lover's hand, passion replaced any anxiety. Their eyes shone with happiness, as Judy pulled Kathleen toward the bedroom.

"I fixed lunch," Kathleen said.

"It'll wait," Judy responded.

The bacon was cold, and the tomatoes warm by the time they claimed the BLTs Kathleen had prepared. Neither woman noticed. They both decided that happiness was the best of all condiments.

About the Kayt

Kayt C. Peck lived the ranch life as a child and young adult and knows the smell, feel, hardships and gratifications of life on the range. The hard-work and determination needed to survive on a Texas farm and ranch helped her as she began a life-long career as a writer that has included working as a journalist, a public-affairs officer in the U.S. Naval Reserve, and as a grants expert writing applications raising over $30 million for worthy domestic and even international organizations. She has published two other novels, one biography, and written a number of plays, including being a two time awardee in the Rocky Mountain Voices play competition. She has authored and published numerous articles, short-stories and poems. Today, she lives quietly in her cabin home in the mountains of northeastern New Mexico.

Other titles available at Sapphire Books

Award winning novel - Always Faithful
ISBN - 978-0-9828608-0-9

Major Nichol "Nic" Caldwell is the only survivor of her helicopter crash in Iraq. She is left alone to wonder why she and she alone. Survivor's guilt has nothing on the young Major as she is forced to deal with the scars, both physical and mental, left from her ordeal overseas. Before the accident, she couldn't think of doing anything else in her life.

Claire Monroe is your average military wife, with a loving husband and a little girl. She is used to the time apart from her husband. In fact, it was one of the reasons she married him. Then, one day, her life is turned upside down when she gets a visit from the Marine Corps.

Can these two women come to terms with the past and finally find happiness, or will their shared sense of honor keep them apart?

Forever Faithful - ISBN - 978-1-939062-75-8

Life is what happens when you make other plans, and Nic and Claire have just found out that life and the Marine Corps have other plans for their lives.

Nic Caldwell has served her country, met the woman of her dreams, and has reached the rank of Lieutenant Colonel. She's studying at one of the nation's most prestigious military universities, setting her sights on a research position after graduation. Things couldn't be better and then it happens; a sudden assignment to Afghanistan derails any thoughts of marriage and wedded bliss. Another combat zone, another tragedy, and Nic suddenly finds herself fighting for her life.

Claire Monroe loves her new life in Monterey. She's finally where she wants to be, getting ready to start her master's program at the local university, watching her daughter, Grace, growing up, and getting ready to marry the love of her life. What could possibly derail a perfect life? The Marine Corps.

Will Nic survive Afghanistan? Can Claire step up and be the strength in their relationship? Or will this overseas assignment and a catastrophic accident divide their once happy home?

The Demon Within - ISBN - 978-1-939062-81-9

What do you do when you're a demon hunter who is also possessed by an ancient demon who needs to feed off other demonic spirits? Where do you turn when that demon's hunger for the deaths of others reaches its apex causing you to become an overzealous killer and murderer of evil? How do you live with yourself night after night as you wade through the detritus that was once a demonic entity destroying human lives? And who can you turn to when your very humanity starts slipping through your fingers as the demon within takes control?

Witches, that's who.

When Denny Silver falls down the rabbit hole of toward a path of her own destruction, only her friends from the local coven have the strength and power to pull her from the darkness...a shadowy blackness that threatens to consume her own soul...a darkness that feeds upon other malevolent forces, transforming her into a mere shade of a human. And as Denny begins losing the battle with her ancient demon, her people, her witches, even her ghost of a best friend rally around her to bolster her humanity and contain the demon that hungers inside of her.

Because Denny Silver is needed.

And if Denny is going to be able to heed the call for help, if she is to become the force that threatens destruction of all things evil, then she must not only learn how to battle her own, she must also be willing to work side-by-side with it. Only by finally accepting who she truly is, can Denny embrace her responsibility as a demon hunter and learn how to control the Demon Within.

Because Denny Silver is needed...and so is her demon.